IT WAS TOO LATE
TO TURN BACK NOW . . .

With a sinking heart, Johnny realized that he would have to go back down through the crypt. There was a high, spike-topped iron fence around the estate, and he didn't feel up to scaling it. But as he turned back toward the dark doorway of the chapel, he saw something. Someone was coming down the steps toward him with arms outstretched. A figure in a yellow raincoat. A figure with hollow mummy eyes and a withered mummy face and clawlike mummy hands. . . .

THE MUMMY, THE WILL, AND THE CRYPT

"Another lovely, funny, frightening thriller readers will thank Bellairs for. . . . Marvelous surprises for everyone except the villains."

—*Publishers Weekly*

"Johnny and his friend, Professor Childermass, are again plunged into another extraordinary adventure. . . . The pace is fast and the suspense is compelling. Readers will find themselves quickly caught up."

—*Booklist*

THE MUMMY,
THE WILL,
AND THE CRYPT

JOHN BELLAIRS

Frontispiece and maps by
Edward Gorey

BANTAM BOOKS
NEW YORK · TORONTO · LONDON · SYDNEY · AUCKLAND

RL 6, 009–013

THE MUMMY, THE WILL, AND THE CRYPT

*A Bantam Book / published by arrangement with
Dial Books for Young Readers*

PRINTING HISTORY

Dial Books edition published November 1983
Bantam Skylark edition / March 1985
7 printings through August 1988

*Skylark Books is a registered trademark of Bantam Books,
a division of Bantam Doubleday Dell Publishing Group, Inc.
Registered in U.S. Patent and Trademark Office and elsewhere.*

ISBN 0-553-15701-9

Published simultaneously in the United States and Canada

*Bantam Books are published by Bantam Books, a division of Bantam
Doubleday Dell Publishing Group, Inc. Its trademark, consisting of the
words "Bantam Books" and the portrayal of a rooster, is Registered
in U.S. Patent and Trademark Office and in other countries. Marca
Registrada. Bantam Books, 666 Fifth Avenue, New York, New York 10103.*

PRINTED IN THE UNITED STATES OF AMERICA

16   15   14   13   12   11   10

For Candice,
a fellow writer and a good friend

The Mummy, the Will,
and the Crypt

CHAPTER ONE

❊

"Professor, can we go home yet? My feet feel like they're gonna fall off."

"No," said the professor firmly. "We can *not* go home yet. We still have two more rooms full of pictures to look at, and then there's Mr. Glomus's office. No doubt there are art treasures in there. And if you are ever going to become a cultivated young man, you are going to have to learn to appreciate great art. So come along. You can rest your tired feet later."

"But, Professor . . ."

"But me no buts, John. If an old coot who's pushing seventy from the wrong side can keep on his feet, so can you. I'd hum a marching song for you, but I'm afraid that guard over there would not be pleased. I'll give you another two minutes to rest, and then we'll have to move on."

Johnny's voice was a despairing wail. *"Two minutes?"*

"Yes, two minutes. And I'll be counting them on my watch. So relax while you can."

Johnny Dixon and Professor Childermass were sitting on a padded bench in a room full of oil paintings by seventeenth-century Dutch masters with names like Rembrandt and Ruysdael and De Hooch. For hours they had been tramping through the rooms in the vast Glomus mansion—rooms full of the paintings, suits of armor, weapons, and art objects that H. Bagwell Glomus had collected during his long life. Mr. Glomus had been able to collect art because he was rich. And he had gotten rich by starting a cereal company.

A real health nut, Mr. Glomus had invented a cereal drink called Glomar. It was black and looked like coffee, but it was made out of wheat. Even though Glomar tasted terrible, people bought it because they wanted to stay healthy. Later Mr. Glomus invented Oaty Crisps, a cereal that was sort of like Kellogg's Corn Flakes. Oaty Crisps really caught on, and soon Mr. Glomus was able to build a large cereal factory in the town of Gildersleeve, Massachusetts. The factory was right across the street from Mr. Glomus's mansion, and Johnny and the professor had toured it earlier in the day.

Johnny sat still and tried to relax while the professor glowered at his pocket watch, mentally ticking off the seconds. They were an odd pair, these two. Johnny was twelve. He was pale, blond, and freckled, wore glasses, and was rather shy. The professor was short, his nose was red and pitted, and he had muttonchop whiskers that sprouted wildly from the sides of his head. The professor looked crabby, and he actually did have a rotten temper. But he was also a very kind man. He lived across the street from Johnny and his grandparents, and as strange as it may seem, he had become the boy's close friend.

Johnny needed friends. He had a bad habit of avoiding other kids his own age, and after a year of living in the town of Duston Heights, Massachusetts, he had only just begun to change. Most of the time—when he was not at home curled up with a book—Johnny preferred being with the professor.

"Well, time's up! On your feet!" The professor barked out this command and stood up. He stuffed his watch into his pants pocket and turned to Johnny.

"Oh, okay!" Johnny groaned. Wincing, he dragged himself up into a standing position.

However, the professor was not in a sympathetic mood. "What's the matter, John?" he said, in a dry, sarcastic tone. "Is it arthritis or tetanus or frostbite?"

Johnny gave the professor a dirty look. "When this is over with, I want a hot fudge sundae," he muttered sullenly. "Can we go get one?"

The professor smiled as he thought of hot fudge. As Johnny well knew, chocolate was one of the professor's obsessions. "Yes, indeed," he answered, nodding agreeably. "I was planning to do that. There is a wonderful ice cream parlor here in Gildersleeve, and they make big gloppy calorie-filled hot fudge sundaes. We will go there —*after* we visit Mr. Glomus's office. So march!"

Mr. Glomus's mansion was built like a castle, and his office was at the top of a tower at the northeast corner. Johnny and Professor Childermass had to walk down a corridor, up a flight of marble steps, down another corridor, and up a curving flight of cast iron steps before they finally got there. The furnishings in the large circular room were heavy and gloomy. There was a grandfather clock and two heavy mahogany cabinets with glass windows. Mr. Glomus's desk was made of paneled oak, and it looked as if it weighed a ton. On top was a clock made of black marble. The chairs were massive, with black leather upholstery, and there was a dark green rug. A row of narrow windows ran all the way around the room, and in the top part of each one was a piece of colored glass. Since it was a sunny day, the light that came in threw circles of red and purple and green and blue light on the floor, the only cheerful things to be seen.

As Johnny and the professor entered the room they suddenly realized that they had walked in on a guided tour. Clustered together near the desk was a small group of elderly men and women. The guide, a rather bored-looking young woman with a portable loudspeaker in her hand, was rattling off a speech that she must have memorized. Her voice had a singsongy rise and fall, and from the expression on her face she might as well have been talking about the price of beef in Argentina.

". . . and so, in the year 1936, although he had acquired great wealth and built up a thriving business, Mr. Glomus became depressed. He worried and stayed awake nights and began acting strangely. His family doctor advised him to try new things to break out of his rut. So Mr. Glomus began to study demonology and witchcraft, reading all the great books that have been written on this rather sinister subject. He took a trip to Europe and came back with some objects that had once been associated with the practice of witchcraft. Some of these may be seen in the small cabinet by the grandfather clock, including the so-called magic mirror that once belonged to Dr. John Dee, the sixteenth-century sorcerer. But, alas, in spite of his newfound hobby Mr. Glomus continued to feel depressed. And on the evening of November 13, 1936, Mr. H. Bagwell Glomus left his office—this very office that you are standing in—and he went home and drank a mixture of strychnine and cognac. The next morning his servants found him dead on the floor of his bedroom."

Several people gasped. The professor smiled knowingly and nudged Johnny in the ribs.

"Pay attention," he whispered. "This next part is really interesting."

"On the morning following Mr. Glomus's death," the guide went on, "a sealed envelope was found on his desk. In the envelope was a note that revealed the startling fact that Mr. Glomus had *not* left a will!"

There were more gasps and cries of "Oh, no!" and "How 'bout that!" One old lady with a raspy, irritating voice spoke up and said, "What happened to all his moolah, then?"

The guide coughed and looked pained. "Mr. Glomus's . . . uh, his money was divided up among his heirs according to the laws of the Commonwealth of Massachusetts. But this is not the end of the story. It seems that soon after Mr. Glomus's death some odd notes were found in his diary. The members of the Glomus family have deduced from them that a will does indeed exist. And they think that Mr. Glomus left behind clues to its whereabouts. The clues are supposedly right here in this very room!"

Immediately everybody in the group began gawking, turning their heads this way and that. But with a smug smile on her face, the guide went on.

"A great effort has been made to keep things in this office *exactly* as they were on the day Mr. Glomus died. And Mrs. Annabelle Glomus, Mr. Glomus's widow, has offered a reward of $10,000 to anyone who can figure out the hiding place of the will." The guide sighed. "Puzzle experts—people who know about cryptograms and codes—have been brought here from all over the world in an attempt to figure out where the mysterious will is hidden. Many have tried, but all have failed. It is generally thought, though, that the clues are to be found among this rather odd collection of objects on the library table over there. If you will all follow me, please."

With a lot of shuffling and whispering, the group followed the guide across the room to a large walnut table. The tourists talked a good deal among themselves about the objects. Some of them snapped pictures. Poor Johnny kept trying to get a good look at the table, but he couldn't see a blessed thing. He was blocked by several people, but most of all by a tall and very fat man who wore a New York Yankees baseball cap.

"Now, then," said the guide, smiling politely, "this concludes our tour. There is another group due to arrive in a very few minutes, so I must ask you to follow me downstairs to the main hall, where souvenirs may be purchased. Thank you."

Muttering and snapping still more pictures, the group filed out of the room. Johnny and the professor stepped aside to let them pass. Now the two of them were alone, with no one blocking their view. Johnny looked around. Although he could peer at the tantalizing objects on the table now, he decided to save that for last. With the professor following close behind, he started on a little tour of the room. There was Mr. Glomus's desk, with its gloomy marble clock and some pens and pencils laid out in a neat row on the dusty green blotter. Johnny's gaze traveled along the curve of the wall, past the grandfather clock. Between two windows was a china closet, and next to it stood the cabinet with the witchcraft collection in it. Farther along the wall were some paintings in heavy gilt frames. One showed a sunset scene in the White Mountains of New Hampshire. Another showed the Hudson River near West Point. Then there were some chairs, a marble bust of Mr. Glomus on a fluted column, and finally the library table with its peculiar assortment of objects. Johnny walked up to the table and stood with arms folded, looking down. At the front of the table was a big sign that said DO NOT TOUCH. Behind the sign in one corner of the table was a very handsome walnut-and-ivory chess set. It stood on a polished wooden board, and the pieces were all lined up the way they are at the start of a game. Next to the chess set lay an old, yellowed Greek newspaper. It was folded neatly in half so that the top part of the front page showed. The large black letters at the top told—Johnny figured—the name of the newspaper:

ΕΘΝΙΚΟΣ ΚΗΡΥΞ

The second word in the title had a circle drawn around it in red ink. The third item on the table was an old, weathered signboard. It was shield-shaped, with a fancy scalloped border at the top. Johnny could see two rusted screw-eyes sticking out of the top of the board, and he figured that the sign had once hung from a crosspiece on a post or on an iron bracket of some kind. The lettering on the sign was faded, but it could be read. It said YE OLDE TEA SHOPPE. That was it—there was nothing else on the table.

The professor stood watching Johnny with amusement. "Well?" he said in a raspy, needling voice. "Have you figured out where Mr. Glomus's will is? You've had oodles of time."

Johnny gave the professor an exasperated glance. "Aw, come on, Professor! You know darned well that nobody could figure this out! Not even if they had a million and a half years to do it!"

The professor grinned and rubbed his chin. "I will admit," he said dryly, "that the puzzle is a tough one. What possible connection can there be between a chess set, a Greek newspaper, and a sign from somebody's tea shop? Of course, there may not be any connection at all. What I mean is, if I were you, I wouldn't beat my brains out over this ridiculous puzzle. As the young lady pointed out, Mr. Glomus was a bit sick in the head at the end of his life. He may have just wanted to irritate his relatives by holding out the possibility that there was a will after all."

Johnny was about to open his mouth to say something when a mean-looking woman with narrow hornrimmed glasses appeared at the door.

"You two will have to leave now," she snapped. "Didn't you hear what the guide said? There's another group due in."

The professor turned to her with a malicious gleam in his eye. He hated bossy, officious people. "Is it your job to be nasty and impolite?" he asked. "Or are you just doing what comes naturally?"

The woman's mouth dropped open, and while she stood there looking astonished, Johnny and the professor walked out past her and down the stairs. As they went, the professor began to chuckle in a self-satisfied way.

A few minutes later Johnny and the professor were sitting in an ice cream parlor that had old-fashioned wooden booths and Tiffany glass lampshades and a marble counter and even a jukebox. The jukebox was playing "Come On-A My House," a song that the professor hated, and he flinched now and then while digging into his hot fudge sundae. Johnny was having a tin roof sundae, which is a hot fudge sundae with peanuts on top. And as he slurped and munched and crunched he felt at peace with the world. But Johnny liked puzzles—chess puzzles and picture puzzles and Chinese puzzles and all the other kinds—and so his mind kept drifting back to Mr. Glomus's office and the mysterious array of objects on the table.

The professor was a shrewd man, and he could tell from the expression on Johnny's face that he was still wrestling with the problem. "Come on, John," he said. "Give it up! It's a puzzle that can't be solved. It's like the Mad Hatter's riddle: *Why is a raven like a writing desk?* There isn't any solution."

Johnny popped a fudge-covered peanut into his mouth. He chewed it slowly and stubbornly. "Professor," he said thoughtfully, "what do you think would *really* happen if somebody found Mr. Glomus's will?"

The professor shrugged. "The law divided up Mr. Glomus's estate among his heirs. His wife and his two worthless sons got some money, and so did his two surviving brothers, and his sister. If a will turned up, there'd be fights in court and yelling and screaming, some reshuffling of the money, and then a lot of hatefulness and ill will. It'd be like setting off a bomb in a fireworks factory."

Johnny laughed at the professor's description. But then he paused. "Hey, wait a minute! If it's gonna cause so much trouble to find the will, how come Mrs. Glomus wants to find it?" he said.

The professor licked his spoon pensively. "Well," he said slowly, "I don't know much about Mrs. Glomus, but I suspect she is one of these fussy, finicky types that think everything in life should come out neatly, with straight edges and all. Rich people are *supposed* to leave wills, and so it may really gripe her to think that her late hubby didn't leave one. Or maybe she's just greedy. She may not be satisfied with the money she got under the present arrangement and may be gambling that she'll get more if a will is found. I don't know. But if I were her, I'd leave things the way they are. If a will is found, she may lose her ten thousand dollars, and more besides."

Suddenly the professor jumped up. "See here, now! I've had enough of chewing over the affairs of the Glomus family. It's time for us to pay up and hit the road, because I have mountains of papers to get through tonight. Term papers! *Arrgh!* Reams and reams of indigestible nonsense! But they have to be done, I suppose. Come on, John. Let's get a move on."

Later, as the car roared on through the twilight toward Duston Heights, Johnny sat slumped in the front seat with his eyes closed. It had been a busy, exciting day, and now the motion of the car, the droning of the motor, and the whiz of passing cars were putting him to sleep.

CHAPTER TWO

~≫•≪~

It was a few weeks later, a chilly night in late September. Johnny was walking home from a Monday night Boy Scout meeting at the Methodist church, wearing his new Boy Scout uniform with the red neckerchief and the bright red-and-white numerals *112* sewed on the right shoulder. For months the professor and Johnny's gramma and grandpa had been trying to persuade him to join. They were worried that Johnny was too much of a loner, and they wanted him to break out of his shell and make some friends. And so he had finally signed up with Troop *112*. The first meeting had not been much. Before the scoutmaster showed up, the boys spent their time horsing around, playing games of Steal the Bacon (using a knotted towel for the bacon) and throwing the cakes of Ivory soap at each other that they were supposed to be carving into little animals and things like that. But when the meeting started and things quieted down a bit, Johnny decided he liked the scoutmaster and most of the other boys too. He was stubborn about changing his mind, but he was beginning to think that maybe—just maybe—this Boy Scout business was a good idea.

As Johnny walked on, all sorts of thoughts came crowding into his mind. He thought about his mother, who had been in her grave for over a year now. He thought about his dad, who was flying a jet for the Air Force, over in Korea. The year was 1951, and the Korean War was raging. Mr. Dixon didn't have to be over there, because he had already served in the Air Force in World War Two. Besides, he was the only surviving parent of a dependent child. But he had volunteered anyway, because he liked flying. Johnny did not understand why his dad wanted to do such a dangerous thing. He didn't understand why the Americans had to go help the South Koreans fight the North Koreans and the Chinese Communists. But he did know one thing— he knew that he was scared. Sometimes before he went to bed at night Johnny would imagine seeing his dad's jet plane hurtling through the sky. Suddenly it would burst, exploding in flame and smoke, with pieces flying everywhere. Johnny would close his eyes and shudder. He worried about his dad a lot. Sometimes when the mail arrived on Saturday afternoons, Johnny wondered if there was an official U.S. government telegram in the pile, a telegram that began *We regret to inform you.* . . .

Johnny wished that he could stop worrying about his dad and just go along with what the professor had told him: There was one big rule in life—the things you worried about never happened, and the things that happened were never the ones you expected. Not that this bit of advice helped Johnny much. It simply meant that he spent more time guessing at what the unexpected disasters in his life would be.

When Johnny started up the walk toward his front door, he was suddenly hit with the chilling feeling that something was wrong. Quickly he glanced toward the big bay window. The window was dark. This was odd, because usually at this time of night Gramma would be in the living room watching TV. The Dixons were poor, and they hadn't had a television set until recently, when Professor Childermass had bought them one as a present. At first Gramma had been suspicious of this newfangled invention, convinced that the rays it emitted were harmful. But before long she was a regular TV addict, watching the *Kate Smith Hour*, Milton Berle, and soap operas like *Search for Tomorrow*. But no gray aquarium glow hovered about the walls tonight. Johnny wondered what Gramma was doing.

Oh, well. She might be up to any number of things. She might be lying down upstairs with a headache—she had had a lot of headaches lately, for some reason. She might be making fudge or a lemon meringue pie in the kitchen. She might be in the bathroom. So Johnny shrugged and started up the steps. *Slam* went the screen door. He walked across the porch and opened the front door. Now he was in the long, musty-smelling hall that ran from the front to the back of the house. With a strong sense of foreboding, Johnny opened the door to the living room and peered in. It was dark. Johnny could see various shapes: the rounded bulk of the brown armchair, the boxy shape of the television set. And as his eyes got used to the dark, he saw his grandmother sitting, rigid and still, on the couch. Her glasses glimmered faintly, but she was not moving a muscle. Terror clutched at Johnny's heart. *What was the matter with her?*

Johnny swallowed several times. When he finally spoke, his voice was weak. "Gramma?"

"Hullo, John. How're you?" Gramma sounded dull and lifeless, like a recording.

Not knowing what to say, Johnny hovered in the doorway. Then Gramma spoke again, unexpectedly, in the same flat voice.

"You're home from school early, arncha? They letcha out early, did they?"

Early. It was nine o'clock at night. Gramma had gone crazy. Or else she was drunk. But, no, she was death on liquor, wouldn't even stay in the same room with people who were drinking. Johnny felt sick. How had this happened? What could he do? He wanted to run out the door yelling and screaming. But instead he stood rooted to the spot. Suddenly he heard footsteps behind him. Somebody was coming up the walk. The sound broke Johnny's trance, and he dashed down the hall to flip the switch that turned on the porch light. When he stepped out onto the porch, he saw his grampa and Professor Childermass. Even in the pale light he could see that their faces were grim and haggard. And Johnny knew in a flash that they too knew something was wrong with Gramma.

The screen door opened, and the two old men entered. Grampa walked slowly forward and put his hand gently on Johnny's shoulder.

"Johnny, we hafta talk to you," he said quietly.

Johnny followed the professor and Grampa through the house to the kitchen. Grampa switched on the kitchen light, closed the door, and went to the stove to turn on the gas under the teakettle. Johnny could see now that Grampa's eyes were red-rimmed, and there were wet streaks on his loose, leathery cheeks. He had been crying.

The professor stood in the middle of the room with his arms folded. He stared hard at the floor. "John," he said, "there is something the matter with your grandmother. I'm sorry you had to come upon her alone like that, but I was across the street with your grampa. He was . . . well, he was terribly upset, as you might imagine."

Johnny's eyes were wide with fear. And now his voice trembled as he spoke. "Professor, what is it? Why . . . why's she actin' that way?"

The professor looked forlornly at Johnny. He opened his mouth to speak, but all he said was "My cousin . . ." Then he snapped his mouth shut suddenly and turned to stare at the wallpaper. His face became a frozen, secretive mask.

Johnny wondered for a second, but then it hit him. He knew what the professor had been about to say: *My cousin Bea died of a brain tumor.* Many times Johnny had heard the professor talking to Grampa about how Cousin Bea had had a brain tumor, only Doc Schermerhorn diagnosed it as bad teeth, so she died. A brain tumor. It sounded so horrible, so hopeless. Johnny hoped that the professor was wrong.

Grampa gently put his hand on Johnny's shoulder. "We called the . . . the hospital," he said in a broken, tearful voice. "The ambulance is comin' to get her."

Johnny looked dully at Grampa. He waited for Grampa to take his hand away, and then he walked over to a kitchen chair and slumped into it. He felt stunned, as if he had been hit on the head with a baseball bat. He couldn't cry. He couldn't feel anything or think anything except *This isn't really happening. It's not real.* In spite of what the professor had said, the things you are afraid of sometimes really *do* happen. And when they do, it feels worse than any nightmare.

The red electric clock over the stove buzzed, but

there was no other sound in the room. Finally the professor coughed. He turned and took Grampa firmly by the arm.

"Come on, Henry," he said in a low voice. "I know it's not going to be any fun, but we have to get Kate ready to go. The ambulance'll be here any minute. The sooner the doctors examine your wife, the sooner they can start fixing her up. She may not know why we want her to go, but . . . well, I don't expect she'll give us a whole lot of trouble. Are you with me?"

Grampa nodded. Then he opened the kitchen door, and he and the professor went out. Johnny followed them timidly through the dining room and the front room to the parlor. The professor went into the darkness, and a few minutes later he came out with Gramma holding on to his arm. She shuffled along uncertainly, and Johnny noticed that she was wearing her blue cloth slippers, the ones with the little blue felt rosettes. Her stockings were wrinkly and saggy, and her face was blank. She looked as if she did not have the slightest idea of what was happening.

The ambulance arrived. It stood in front of the house with its red light flashing. Two attendants got out and took a wheeled cot out of the back of the vehicle. They helped Gramma down the front steps, gently eased her onto the cot, and wheeled the cot out to the ambulance. Gramma was lifted inside, and the rear doors were closed. The big white vehicle roared away, its siren screaming. The professor watched it go for a second, and then he went across the street to get his car—he was going to drive Grampa to the hospital. As he was about to leave the house, Grampa turned to Johnny and asked him if he wanted to go with them. But Johnny said no, he would stay home. He stood in the doorway watching as the car backed out of the driveway and rolled away down the street.

While Gramma was in the hospital the days passed in a blur for Johnny. During school he had a hard time keeping his mind on his work because he was thinking about her so much. He told Sister Mary Anthony, his eighth grade teacher, about what had happened, and she asked the whole class to pray for Johnny's grandmother. And each day, after school had let out, Johnny went into the gloomy, echoing church next door and lit a candle in front of the Blessed Virgin's altar. Kneeling at the altar rail, he prayed that nothing bad would happen to his gramma.

Finally the news came. Yes, Gramma had a brain tumor. The doctor at the hospital explained to Johnny and Grampa that there were two kinds of tumors, benign and malignant. A benign tumor was just a little lump in the brain. It might grow, but it usually wouldn't do any harm. A malignant tumor would grow and eventually kill the patient. Unfortunately you couldn't tell if a tumor was benign or malignant until you actually operated and took it out. The doctor was an honest sort of person, and he laid it on the line: It was going to be a dangerous operation, especially for someone as old as Gramma was. Something might go wrong, or they might not get all of the tumor out. Everybody would just have to sit tight.

Grampa drove Johnny home after the session with the doctor. Neither of them said a word until the car had stopped in the driveway and Grampa muttered, "Gotta go fix supper." Then he got out of the car, closed the door, and loped off toward the house. Johnny watched him go. Grampa looked utterly defeated. His shoulders sagged, and his head hung. Tears came to Johnny's eyes, but with a snorting sound and a shudder he forced the sobs down. He got out of the car and was starting to walk down the driveway to the garage when he heard someone call.

"John! Over here!"

Johnny turned. It was the professor. He was standing in his front yard with a golf club in his hand. The professor played a perfectly terrible game of golf, but he kept at it anyway. Sometimes he practiced his swing in his backyard with a little plastic practice ball. The practice swings didn't help his game any, but—as he often said, sourly—he had chopped some lovely big holes in his back lawn.

"Johnny! Come here a minute. Can I talk to you?"

Johnny walked back up the driveway and across the street.

"Yeah, Professor? Whaddaya want?" The tone of his voice showed how rotten he felt.

The professor smiled sadly. "Is it as bad as all that?" he asked.

Johnny nodded gloomily. "It sure is. We talked to the doctor and he said—"

"Yes. I know. I called up the doctor earlier and got a full report. It's awful, I know, but . . . well, let's hope everything will turn out okay."

"Fat chance," said Johnny bitterly. He was in such a black mood that he did not want to be cheered up, and he did not want the professor to be painting fake rosy pictures for him.

"John," said the professor gravely, and he walked closer to the boy. He put his arm around him and smiled in a pained way. "I think you need to get away from here. I think you need to go on a vacation."

CHAPTER THREE

꧁•꧂

Johnny was stunned—stunned, shocked, and angry. It was as if the professor had said, *Come on! Let's throw a party!* When he tried to speak, Johnny found that all he could do was splutter and stammer.

"Professor, I . . . I mean how could you . . . with, with, you know. . . ."

The professor was unmoved. He did not act as if he had said anything outrageous. "I mean it, John. It may sound a bit unlikely to you right now, but . . . well, tell you what. After supper I'm going to be making a cake, and I'd appreciate some kitchen help. Why don't you come over after you've eaten, and I'll explain my immodest proposal, okay?"

Johnny just stared at the professor. He was genuinely puzzled. He knew that the professor was not a hard or unfeeling person. Maybe when he had explained what he had on his mind, it would all make sense. "Okay," he said hesitantly. "I'll . . . I'll come over later." And Johnny turned abruptly and walked back to the house.

Supper that night was really pretty awful. It was another example of grampa's horrible cooking: the hamburgers were not only overdone, they were charred. Instead of mashed potatoes there was a slice of Wonder bread. And the canned peas had been cooked so long that they tasted like mushy green spit wads. After one bite of the hamburger Johnny went out to the kitchen cupboard and brought out all the sauces and condiments he could find: A-1 sauce, ketchup, mustard, and Heinz 57 sauce. And with the aid of these he managed to choke the food down. Grampa never said a word all through the meal. It was painful just to look at him. As soon as he could, Johnny excused himself and went across the street.

When Johnny arrived, the professor was all done up in one of his chef's outfits—a big white apron and a puffy white hat. On the kitchen table were boxes of flour and sugar, a bottle of milk, a can of baking powder, and some tiny bottles of vanilla extract and artificial food coloring. In front of the professor was a big green crockery bowl with some creamy yellow cake mixture in it. When he saw Johnny, the professor looked up quickly and grinned. Using a big wooden spoon, he began to stir the batter.

"Now, then," he said brusquely, "where were we? Ah, yes. I was trying to convince you to go away for a while. Do you want to know why? Well, it's all very simple. You're not doing your gramma any good by being here. You may think that you are, but you're not. If you go to visit her in the hospital, you'll find that she's in a rather strange state. And after the operation she'll be sleeping a lot. When you're at home, you'll see that your grampa is not much fun to be with. The two of you will just sit around making each other moody."

The professor paused. He dipped his finger into the raw batter, came up with a big sticky glob, and put it in his mouth. The professor had a passion for raw cake batter. "So, John," he went on as he stirred, "I think you should go somewhere. As you know, next week is Massachusetts State Physical Fitness Week."

Johnny was dumbfounded. What was the connection between Physical Fitness Week and going on a vacation? Between October 1 and 7 the kids in all the grade schools in the state would go to lectures and slide shows and movies and panel discussions on physical fitness instead of attending classes. In Duston Heights there would be special events like relay races and baseball and tug-of-wars every day out at the athletic field. All this left Johnny cold. He was not a big athlete. He could just barely play softball, but not well enough to please the tough kids who ran things on the St. Michael's

School playground. At all other sports he was a complete washout. And so he was expecting to spend Physical Fitness Week standing on the sidelines and watching other kids have fun.

"Yeah," Johnny said sullenly. "I know all about Physical Whoozis Week. What the heck does that have to do with going someplace on a vacation?"

The professor held up a gooey forefinger. "It has this to do with it, my fine feathered friend! As part of the big whoopy-doo of this wonderful week a group of Boy Scouts from this area is going to take a bus trip up into the White Mountains, to a scout camp near Lake Chocorua. When they get there, they're going to spend a glorious, delightful week hiking along mountain trails and singing around campfires and having a grand time. You'll enjoy it—I know you will. And it'll be a million times better than moping around at home. What do you say, eh? Can I twist your arm?"

Johnny looked doubtful. The whole thing sounded like it would be fun, but, well, he didn't think he ought to be having fun right now. It would be like going to a movie on the afternoon of someone's mother's funeral.

"I don't think Grampa would want me to go," he said.

The professor snorted and added a handful of sugar to the batter. "Oh, yes, he would. He might deny it, but at this point I think he'd be extremely glad to have you somewhere else for a short time."

Johnny picked up the measuring spoons and clacked them together. He was really torn. He liked the Boy

Scouts, and he loved the White Mountains. And hiking was something he could do.

"It'd cost a lot of money, wouldn't it?"

"Oh, I'll pay for it," said the professor, shrugging carelessly. "What's the use of having money in the bank if you can't do something nice with it? Now, come on. Be a good sport and say yes."

Johnny was still uncertain, and since the professor had decided that no more good would come of coaxing and wheedling, they agreed that Johnny would think about the professor's plan until tomorrow.

Johnny stayed and helped the professor with his baking. The cake came out perfectly, and after the professor made Ma Perkins's Own Spice Frosting, the two of them sat down to gobble. Then the professor went back across the street with Johnny and half of the cake on a plate inside an aluminum cake carrier. Johnny went up to his room to read while the professor sat down to talk to his old friend Grampa Dixon. He wanted to visit with Grampa to cheer him up. And of course he also wanted to do a little persuading.

A few days later, on Sunday, October 1, Johnny was riding northward in a school bus full of Boy Scouts. In the metal rack above his seat was a backpack, his cardboard suitcase, and his sleeping bag. Johnny was wearing his Boy Scout uniform, and all around him were other boys in uniform. They had just finished singing "Ninety-eight Bottles of Beer on the Wall," the song that is calculated to drive bus drivers out of their minds. Now, while most of the boys were talking and laughing and pestering each other, Johnny sat quietly, staring at the ring binder filled with notes on his lap. On the seat next to him was an illustrated guidebook from the Glomus mansion. He was working on the Glomus puzzle, trying to make sense out of the objects on the late cereal king's office table. He didn't really expect to solve the mystery; this was just something he had brought along to pass the time. As usual, Johnny was approaching the whole thing logically, trying to list all the qualities of the objects on the table, but oddly enough, logic wasn't helping him much.

CHESS SET
Material: wood and ivory
Arrangement: just the way it is before a game starts.
Design: Staunton

NEWSPAPER
Language: Greek
Material: coarse paper known as newsprint
Lettering of headline: large black letters in Greek
alphabet. Word circled in red is KHPYΞ. It means
"herald." Whole title EΘNIKOΣ KHPYΞ
means NATIONAL HERALD.

SIGNBOARD
Material: wood. Don't know what kind.
Notes: Wood is pretty beat up. Probably was
outdoors for a long time. Blue letters say
YE OLDE TEA SHOPPE.

Johnny looked glumly at the orderly list that he had made. No, it was not much help. On the other hand, he was proud of what he had been able to find out about this curious collection of things. The guidebook had helped a lot. It had a close-up color picture of the table with the puzzle on it, and another close-up photo of the Greek newspaper. The professor had told Johnny the meaning of the Greek words. And Johnny himself had added the information about the Staunton design. Johnny was a chess nut, and he knew that the Staunton design was the most common. All this information was fine, just fine, except for one tiny little thing: It didn't bring Johnny any closer to solving the puzzle.

Johnny sighed. He picked up the guidebook that lay beside him and began to leaf absentmindedly through it. He looked again at the picture of the table with its mysterious collection of objects. This was all he had to go on. It would have been nice if he could have popped back to Gildersleeve, where the mansion was, before the bus trip began. But Gildersleeve was forty miles from Duston Heights—the trip would've taken too much time. Still, it would have been nice to have another look at the clues. *Clues, shmooze!* he said to himself as he slammed the book shut and threw it back down on the seat. The professor was probably right. The puzzle was a cruel, pointless joke. It could not be solved and was not meant to be solved. It was just something that Mr. Glomus had whipped up to drive his family crazy. Why was Johnny so interested in this idiotic puzzle, anyway?

Was it just because he liked difficult mental challenges? No, there was something else too: There was the reward. Ten thousand dollars for anyone who could figure out the hiding place of the will. He would use the money to pay for Gramma's operation. Johnny knew that operations were expensive. Gramma and Grampa were poor.

There was one more reason why Johnny was going after the will: Like a lot of people, he was always hoping that someday he would get to do something terribly distinguished and exciting, like finding a lost city buried under the sands of Egypt. The Glomus will was like a lost city to Johnny. If he found it, he would get a reward, he would become famous, and he would be able to do something wonderfully generous and kind for his grandparents. What more could anyone ask?

Johnny gazed dreamily out the window of the bus. The mountains were getting closer. In the distance, on the horizon, he could see long rumpled gray and blue lines. Lazily Johnny leaned back in his seat and wondered what the week at Camp Chocorua would be like.

CHAPTER FOUR

※•※

Lake Chocorua looks as if it had been intended by God to be a mirror for noble Mount Chocorua. And Mount Chocorua deserves a mirror, because it is a mountain that has *presence*. It stands out. Most of the White Mountains of New Hampshire have been worn down by millions of years of wind and weather into gently rounded, tree-covered humps. But at the top of Mount Chocorua a sharp horn of rock thrusts up into the sky. When Johnny first saw it, the mountain was at its most beautiful. It was the height of the fall foliage season, and the maple trees that grow on the mountain's sides were lit up with brilliant reds and oranges. Johnny looked up and hoped for a day when the wind wouldn't blow, so that he would see Mount Chocorua perfectly reflected in the still waters of its own special lake.

The bus followed New Hampshire State Route 16 past the mountain and the lake onto a dirt road that branched off from the highway. It crossed a rickety wooden bridge until it came to a wooded area where rich people had their summer homes.

In a clearing in the middle of a big patch of wooded land stood Camp Chocorua, which consisted of four two-story log buildings and a flagpole. Johnny and the other boys were assigned their bunks in these buildings. That night a fire was made in the big brick fireplace in one of the dormitory buildings, and the boys and the counselors gathered around to sing songs and tell ghost stories and eat popcorn and drink cider. The next day the camp routine would begin.

On Tuesday morning, after breakfast, Johnny was hiking up a dusty road with a group of other boys. Everybody was in uniform, and Mr. Brentlinger, the head counselor, led the way. Mr. Brentlinger was a big, hulking, rather kindly man who loved to sing songs. As they tramped along, raising clouds of yellow dust, they sang "We're on the Upward Trail," "The Happy Wanderer," and the ever-popular Army hiking song, "Sound Off!" It was a warm day, and Johnny was happy. Here he was, with kids who talked and joked and played games with him. It felt good, and he didn't want it to end.

Around noon the hikers stopped for lunch. The place

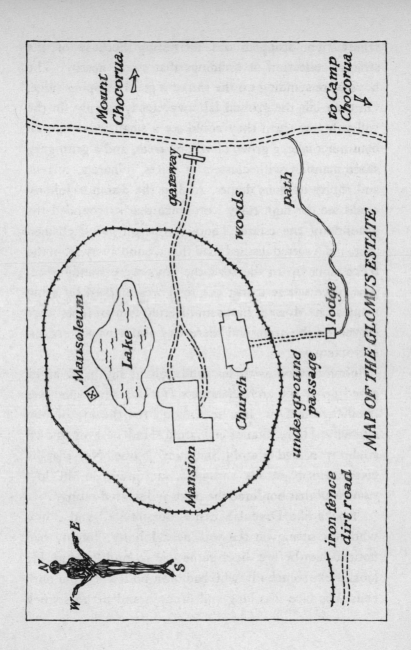

MAP OF THE GLOMUS ESTATE

Mount Chocorua

to Camp Chocorua

gateway

woods

path

lodge

underground passage

Church

Mansion

Lake

Mausoleum

N
E
W
S

—×—×— iron fence
--------- dirt road

where they stopped was interesting because of the strange collection of buildings that stood nearby. The boys were standing on the rim of a gently sloping ridge. On their left the ground fell away fairly steeply. In the valley below them they could see a small stone church by a quiet lake, a grove of willow trees, and a grim gray stone mansion with clusters of spires, minarets, turrets, and funny bulbous domes. And in the distance Johnny could see the high rusty iron fence that surrounded the grounds of the estate. There were iron gates, chained shut, and a rutted disused road that wound away from the fence right up to the road the boys were standing on. The place where it met the road was marked by a big stone arch. Monster heads and leering human faces were carved on the arch, and there was also a name: STAUN-TON HAROLD.

Johnny stood with his sandwich in his hand as he gazed up at the arch. *Staunton Harold.* The name was familiar, somehow, but he couldn't for the life of him say why. Hmm. Staunton Harold. Had he ever known anybody named Harold Staunton? Nope. Not that he could remember. He shrugged, sat down on the low stone wall that bordered the road, and started eating.

"Looks like Dracula's castle, doesn't it?" said a boy who was sitting on the wall near Johnny. Johnny had noticed him before, because he was so odd-looking. He looked like somebody who had been pulled at from both ends. His face was long and droopy, and his ears stuck out. He had a long, blunt-ended nose and greasy, curly black hair. His gangly arms hung down, and his legs were long too. His feet were enormous. The shoes he was wearing were the kind that kids call gunboats. The boy was eating a huge ham-and-cheese sandwich, and when he stopped chewing, his mouth curled up into a friendly, sarcastic grin.

"What's your name?" he asked.

Johnny smiled shyly. "John Dixon. What's yours?"

The boy grimaced. "Byron Ferguson, believe it or not. But I wish you'd call me Fergie, on account of nobody in their right mind wants to be called Byron." Fergie took another bite of his sandwich. He chewed meditatively and jerked his thumb at the cluster of buildings. "You own this place?"

Johnny stared for a second, but then he realized that the kid was joking. "Oh, sure," he said, grinning. "It's all mine, and I'm Count Dracula. I eat and chew with the lower intestinal tract! I bite the head from the body and suck the blood! Born in Madagascar in 1892! Shot dead and come to life again!" This last part was a sideshow barker's routine that Johnny's dad had memorized and recited so many times that it had worn a groove in Johnny's memory.

Fergie laughed and spat bits of sandwich across the grass. "Where the heck'd you learn *that*?"

Johnny shrugged. "Oh, I know lots of things like that. I know poems and weird facts and all kinds of stuff."

Fergie turned to him suddenly. There was a gleam in his eye. "What happened to the Colossus of Rhodes?" he asked.

Johnny was startled. All he knew was that the Colossus of Rhodes was a huge bronze statue that had been one of the Seven Wonders of the World at one time and that it wasn't around anymore.

"Time's up," snapped Fergie. He grinned triumphantly. "Don't know? Well, it fell down during an earthquake and got sold to a Saracen junk dealer."

Johnny's eyes narrowed. He was not going to take this lying down. "Name the eight guys who killed Julius Caesar," he said.

This one stumped Fergie. He said he didn't know, and Johnny proudly rattled off the eight Roman names. Fergie looked at him with admiration, and Johnny realized that they were going to become friends.

Fergie and Johnny talked a blue streak to each other all during the rest of the hike. Johnny told Fergie about the professor, and about his dad, and Gramma's upcoming operation. At dinnertime that night the two boys met outside the door of the dining hall so they could get a seat together and talk some more. Tonight dinner consisted of hot dogs on buns, potato chips, baked beans, and "bug juice"—otherwise known as Kool-Aid. Soon Fergie and Johnny were seated across from each other at one of the long tables. They talked about baseball. Since Johnny wore glasses, he was naturally an expert on bespectacled players. Dom DiMaggio was a special favorite of his, and he had been to Red Sox games at Fenway Park, where the kids chanted:

He's better than his brother Joe,
Do-mi-nic Di-Mag-gi-o!

Next the boys went on to players who had other disabilities. Like Monty Stratton, who pitched with a wooden leg, and Mordecai Brown of the Cubs, who had only three fingers on his pitching hand. But in the midst of all this odd-fact fun, Johnny suddenly grew thoughtful and silent.

Fergie stared. " 'Smatter? Somethin' on your mind?"

"Yeah. I keep thinkin' about that name on that stone arch. It . . . well, it kinda reminds me of somethin'. I dunno what, though."

Fergie shrugged. "Well, it'll come to you in the middle of the night. That's what my mom always says."

Johnny mumbled "Yeah" and went on thinking about Staunton Harold. Later, after dinner, he went to the rec room with Fergie and played a couple of games of chess. Then, around ten, he dragged his weary, aching body up to his room. Johnny had a double room that he shared with a fat, obnoxious kid named Duane Eckelbecker, or "Double-decker" Eckelbecker, as he was known. When Johnny walked in, he found Eckelbecker sprawled on his cot, reading a comic book.

"H'lo, Duane," he said.

Eckelbecker grunted. He flipped a page and went on reading.

Johnny sat down on his cot and picked up the blue binder that had his Glomus puzzle stuff inside. He reached over to the bureau drawer and dug out a sheaf of letter paper and some envelopes. Then, using the blue binder as a desk, Johnny started writing. He wrote a letter to his grandmother in the hospital and another to his grandfather and one to the professor. In his letter to Grampa, he asked if Gramma was okay and when the operation was going to be. Then he folded the letters neatly, put them into the envelopes, and got out the address list that was tucked into a pocket inside the front cover of the binder. But just as he was beginning to address the first letter, he stopped. His pen halted in midstroke.

He had thought of something.

Quickly Johnny flipped open the binder. His eyes traveled down the page. *Chess Set . . . Design: Staunton.* Then, farther down the page, Johnny found the word in the Greek newspaper that was circled in red. The word *KHPYΞ*, which meant "herald."

Staunton. Herald. Staunton Harold.

What did it mean? Was it all a crazy coincidence? Johnny's mind began to race madly. Then suddenly he jumped up. There was something he had to know. Eckelbecker looked at Johnny with sluggish curiosity as he raced for the door, opened it, and slammed it behind him.

With the binder still in his hands, Johnny ran downstairs to the dining room. The huge room was mostly dark, but a fire was crackling in the big brick fireplace, and shadows danced over the trophies and drinking mugs that littered the stone mantelpiece. In a big leather armchair before the fire sat Mr. Brentlinger. His legs were stretched out comfortably in front of him, and he was puffing on a big briar pipe. When Johnny saw Mr. Brentlinger, he paused. He was scared of counselors and teachers and policemen and other grown-ups who had authority over him. On the other hand, he knew that Mr. Brentlinger was a very nice, easygoing guy. And Johnny also knew that he would go out of his mind if he didn't find out the things that he wanted to know.

Cautiously Johnny walked forward until he was standing near the armchair. He coughed, and suddenly Mr. Brentlinger became aware of his presence. He turned his head and spewed out a long, thin stream of pipe smoke.

"Hi, John. It is John, isn't it?"

Johnny nodded tightly. "Yes, sir. That's my name."

"I thought it was. Well, John, what can I do for you?"

He's gonna think this is crazy, thought Johnny. But he plunged ahead. "Uh . . . well . . . Mr. Brentlinger, could . . . could you . . . I mean, would you happen to know the name of the people who own that old mansion that's near the place where we ate our lunch? You know, with the towers on it and the little church next door to it? I was just kinda . . . well, interested in knowing."

Mr. Brentlinger turned and looked at Johnny. He laughed and shook his head. "Well, now! That *is* a strange thing to be asking. Were you hoping that the place was haunted or something?"

Johnny squirmed and clutched the binder tightly against his chest. He began to think that it had been a mistake to bring it with him. What if Mr. Brentlinger wanted to see what was inside? Would he laugh and decide that Johnny was a Grade-A lunatic? "I just wondered if you knew," he mumbled. Johnny could feel his face turning red.

Mr. Brentlinger looked at Johnny sympathetically. "I wasn't trying to make fun of you, John," he said gently. "I just couldn't resist having my little joke. Actually I think I do remember who owns that place. It's the family that owns the cereal company. You know, the people that make Oaty Crisps and all that other gunk. They have a really weird name. It's Glomfield or Glimp or something like that. Anyway, it was the old man, the founder of the business, that built the place. It's falling down now—the mansion, I mean, and I keep wondering what they're gonna *do* with the place. I wish I could remember that name for you. Hmm . . . hmm . . . let me think a bit. . . ."

Mr. Brentlinger went on hmming and puffing at his pipe. Johnny stood there in the darkness, trembling. He felt cold all over, but he also felt wildly triumphant. He had doped out the puzzle—part of it, anyway. Could he be wrong? Johnny didn't think so. The lost Glomus will was out here, out in that old mansion—or somewhere near it maybe. Johnny wanted to do eighteen things at once. He wanted to rush out and find a phone and tell the professor what he had discovered. He wanted to tell his new friend, Fergie, and he wanted to be out at the mansion, prowling around.

Mr. Brentlinger's voice broke in on Johnny's thoughts. "Nope, I just can *not* come up with that name! Anything else I can do for you, John? John? Are you there?"

Mr. Brentlinger turned his head and peered into the darkness behind his chair. Johnny was there, all right. At least his body was there. His mind was out among the crumbling stones of the Staunton Harold estate.

"Huh?" said Johnny, startled. "Uh . . . yes, sir . . . er, I mean, what did you say, Mr. Brentlinger?"

Mr. Brentlinger chuckled. "Never mind. So is there anything else I can do for you?"

"Uh . . . no. No, sir," Johnny said. He felt flustered, and he was looking for an exit line. "You told me what I wanted to know, so . . . so I guess I'll go up to bed now. Thanks a lot."

"Don't mention it. Sleep tight."

Johnny went up to his bedroom, but he did not go to sleep. He felt like a wound-up spring. Mechanically he put on his pajamas and went down the hall to brush his teeth and wash his face. Then he came back and crawled into bed, where he lay tossing and turning all night while Eckelbecker snored like a chain saw. If the human brain were a machine with an on-off button, Johnny would have shut his mind off, and he would have gotten some sleep. But he kept thinking about the objects on the table in Mr. Glomus's office. That signboard—what did it mean? Was the will hidden in a teapot? Johnny tossed and turned and moaned.

Finally the room got lighter, and Johnny heard the bugler blasting away, playing reveille outside his window. It was time to get up.

CHAPTER FIVE

❧●❧

Somehow Johnny stumbled through the early morning routine at Camp Chocorua. He washed up, pulled on his clothes, combed his hair, and staggered out to the flag-raising ceremony that always began the day. The skin of his face felt prickly, and he was nervous. But one thing was perfectly clear to him. Before the morning was over, he had to get to a phone so he could talk to the professor. He was dying to tell him about the discovery he had made, and he also wanted very much to know how Gramma was doing.

After the flag had been raised, the boys were dismissed. The orderly khaki-and-red lines broke up into a mob of boys running madly. Johnny tried to fight his way up to the flagpole so he could catch Mr. Brentlinger before he got away, but it was like trying to go up a staircase when everybody else is going down. Stubbornly battling his way forward, he finally reached it, just as Mr. Brentlinger was leaving.

"Mr. Brentlinger? Sir? Can I talk to you for just a minute?"

The head counselor turned and eyed Johnny curiously. He chuckled and shook his head. "Okay, Dixon, what is it now? I think I oughta charge you a fee for services above and beyond the call of duty."

Johnny was flustered. He paused and pulled himself together so he could ask his question. "Sir . . . I'd . . . I'd like to use a phone, if I may. I need to make a long-distance call, but it'd be a collect call. It wouldn't cost the camp any money."

Mr. Brentlinger looked pained. "Oh, God. You *would* ask for *that*! Dixon, look. There's kind of a problem about phones. This whole deal of having the camp open for this week, it was, well, kind of a spur-of-the-moment idea. The place was all shut down, and we had to turn the lights and the gas and everything back on. And you know how there's always something that doesn't get done? Well, the phone didn't get reconnected. Sooo . . . we're out here without a phone. How about that?"

Johnny's heart sank. He felt helpless and horribly frustrated. What was he going to do now?

"*However*," Mr. Brentlinger added, "there is a solution to this dilemma. In about five minutes I have to make a trip into town to mail some letters and make a few phone calls of my own. I use the public phone at the Squam House, which is the hotel in town. Mrs. Woodley knows me, and she'd be glad to let you make a call. So would you like to ride in with me?"

Johnny nodded happily. His problem was solved.

"Town" turned out to be Kancamagus Center, a small village about two miles down Route 16. It had a few side streets with comfortable-looking white clapboard houses, and a main street with a post office, a couple of stores, a gas station, a movie theater called the Scenic, an Odd Fellows Hall, and a white wooden church with a stubby square steeple. These buildings stood along one side of a grassy village common. On the other side of the common was the Squam House. It was a long, two-story structure with green shutters and a porch that ran across its entire front. There were rocking chairs on the porch, and there was a white sign by the steps. The sign said TOURIST ACCOMMODATIONS. *Reasonable Rates*. B. Woodley, proprietor.

Mr. Brentlinger and Johnny went to the post office first. Then they walked across the common to the Squam House. The lobby was deserted except for a young man who was sitting in an easy chair, reading a newspaper. As Johnny passed the man he stopped short. He had seen the man before. But where? He couldn't for the life of him remember. Even though Johnny had always been taught that staring was impolite, he couldn't stop himself. At first the young man tried to ignore him, but finally he put his paper down and gave Johnny a dirty look. He had pale blond eyebrows and frazzled reddish hair, hooded eyes, and a receding chin. He looked secretive, and he looked mean.

Johnny glanced quickly away and walked across the lobby to join Mr. Brentlinger, who was standing at the desk and talking with the proprietor, a fussy-looking old lady with her white hair pulled back in a bun. As she talked the lady pointed off to her left. There was the phone, a scarred black thing in one corner that stood on an antique table with bowed legs. Next to the phone was a skinny blue glass vase that looked like it would tip over if you breathed on it, and there was a funny little stool to sit on. Johnny almost groaned aloud. He had expected a regular phone booth with folding doors. He had wanted to make this a very private conversation, but that was not going to be possible.

Mr. Brentlinger told Johnny that he could use the phone for a long-distance call, as long as it was collect. Also he had to keep it brief, as Mrs. Woodley did not like to have people tying up the phone for too long. So Johnny went and sat in one of the easy chairs in the middle of the room while Mr. Brentlinger made his calls. He was staring aimlessly around the room, when—quite suddenly—he realized that the unpleasant young man was staring at him over the top of his newspaper. And the stare was not just curious, it was hateful. Johnny was startled. What did this creepy-looking guy have against him? Nervously Johnny snatched up an old copy of *Yankee* magazine from a little table and hid behind it.

Time passed. Finally Mr. Brentlinger was through with the phone, and Johnny got to use it. Soon the phone was ringing down in the professor's house in Duston Heights.

When the professor answered, he was in an exceptionally crabby mood. He had been defrosting his refrigerator, which was something that he absolutely hated to do. For about an hour he had been putting pans of boiling water inside the refrigerator and poking at the ice with his Knights of Columbus sword, while cursing loudly, fervently, and picturesquely. Now waves of crankiness were sweeping over him, and he was trying hard to make himself cheerful again.

"Hello," he snapped. "Who is it?"

The voice at the other end was timid and apologetic. "It's me, Johnny. I . . . I need to talk to you."

"John, why the devil are you whispering? Are you involved in a conspiracy? Is the FBI after you?"

Johnny explained that he was sitting out in the open in a hotel lobby.

"So what?" rasped the professor. "Do you have government secrets to pass on? What the blazes do you have to say that's so private?"

Johnny swallowed hard several times. His face got red, and the palms of his hands were sweaty. When people crabbed at him, he always became very flustered.

"I . . . I j-just wanted to t-talk to you for a m-minute," he stammered. "Is . . . is that okay?"

The professor calmed down. He knew about Johnny's problems, and he was sorry he had been such a bear a moment before. "Go ahead," he said, mildly. "I'm listening. Shoot."

"Well, I . . . first of all I just wanted to know how Gramma is. Have they operated on her yet?"

"Yes, they have. She had her operation on Monday night, and she is doing reasonably well, considering her age and everything. The doctors think that they got the whole tumor out, and it was malignant, I'm sorry to say. I'd be lying if I said that I thought that everything was going to be rosy from now on: there may be problems."

"Problems?" Johnny's heart sank.

"Yes, problems. There's always the possibility that the doctors didn't get the whole tumor out, and if that was the case . . . well, it'd be pretty bad. Also, there's your grampa. He's still fairly depressed, and it may be some time before he's his old bouncy self again. So there! I've given you the news, and it's mostly good. Do you have anything else that you want to discuss with me?"

Once again Johnny was hesitant. He looked around nervously and then said in a loud whisper, "I found out something about Mr. Glomus's will!"

The professor groaned. He clenched his fists and struggled against the urge to chew Johnny out. "John," he said through his teeth, "you are supposed to be *en-*

) 50 (

joying yourself! You are supposed to be tramping about on woodland paths among the autumnal splendors of the White Mountains! What on *earth* are you doing thinking about dear old Mr. Glomus's will?"

Johnny explained. He told the professor about the arch that said Staunton Harold, and he told him why he thought the puzzle on the table fit in with it.

". . . and so I think that will just has to be on that old estate somewhere," Johnny went on breathlessly. "Don't you think I must be right?"

The professor was silent for so long that Johnny was afraid they had been cut off.

"Professor? Hello? Hello? Are you there?"

"Yes, I'm here," said the professor in a strained, testy voice. "But if I were *there*, I'd be driving you into the ground like a tent stake! John, this puzzle solution of yours is terribly ingenious, but it is absolutely cockeyed! *Please* put it out of your mind and go back to hiking and . . . and whatever else you're supposed to be doing! Do you hear me?"

"But the place out here really does belong to the Glomuses!" said Johnny desperately. "It—"

"I don't care if it belongs to Nebuchadnezzar or Czar Nicholas the Second!" roared the professor, cutting him off. "Let us change the subject! Enjoy yourself! Go out and hike till your feet are sore! Collect autumn leaves and put them into albums! Do anything, but please get your mind off that idiotic will! That is an order!"

"Yes, sir," said Johnny, meekly. He wanted to argue,

but he knew it would be no use. So he promised the professor that he would really try to enjoy himself, and then he said good-bye.

After Johnny had hung up, he looked around. First he turned toward the chair where the creepy young man had been sitting. He was delighted to see that the man was gone. Then Johnny noticed that Mrs. Woodley was standing, stock-still, behind the hotel desk. She was glowering at him. Johnny wondered if everybody in this hotel was crazy. First there was the young man, and now this old bat was making ugly faces at him, even though he hadn't done anything. Johnny happened to glance at the skinny blue glass vase that stood next to the phone. *She thinks I'm gonna smash it*, he said to himself. He had half a mind to knock the vase over and then catch it quickly before it broke, just to see what Mrs. Woodley would do. But most of all he wanted to get out of this creepy hotel as quickly as he could.

Johnny hurried across the lobby, down the front steps, and out into the autumn sunshine. As he crossed the common he thought about the phone conversation he had just had. He felt frustrated, but in an odd way he also felt relieved. He was glad to know that Gramma's operation was over, and that it had been a success. As for the puzzle business, it was true that the professor had not taken him seriously, but at least he had said what he wanted to say. And maybe the professor was right after all. Maybe Johnny should just forget about

Staunton Harold and the Glomus will, shove the whole stupid mess out of his mind.

Mr. Brentlinger's station wagon was parked outside the post office, but Mr. Brentlinger was not there. Probably he was still shopping or chewing the fat with some friend of his. Johnny started to get into the car and wait for him, but as soon as he opened the car door, he noticed something lying on the seat. It was a small square of heavy white paper with ragged edges. Carelessly Johnny picked the paper up and turned it over. What he saw was an old-fashioned black-and-white woodcut. It showed some young men drinking in a tavern. Outside the tavern door stood a skeleton. It held a spear up over its head, and it looked like it was getting ready to throw the spear at the young men. Underneath the picture was a little two-line poem, printed in old-fashioned lettering. It read:

> While Youth do chear
> DEATH may be near

CHAPTER SIX

Johnny sat rigid and still. He felt cold creeping over his body, as if he were slowly turning into a block of ice. The square of paper had been left on the car seat by someone who wanted him to find it. The drawing was familiar to him—in a hazy way. He had seen it in a history book somewhere. And its meaning seemed very clear to Johnny: It was a death threat. But who was threatening him? And why?

Suddenly Johnny looked up. Through the windshield he could see Mr. Brentlinger walking down the sidewalk toward the car. Johnny made a very quick decision. He scrunched the drawing up into a ball in his hand and stuffed it into his pants pocket. He really did not want to discuss this with Mr. Brentlinger or to be told that the drawing was just an ad for a Halloween dance or a free gift from somebody's funeral parlor. He had had enough of calm, reasonable advice from the professor. All he wanted was time to think and figure out what to do.

When the station wagon pulled into the parking lot at Camp Chocorua, Johnny thanked Mr. Brentlinger, got out of the car, and ran up to his room to get his baseball glove. Johnny had seen the kids playing softball as he rode back along the road toward the camp. He loved to play, even though he was not very good at it. And he was always hoping that somehow, mysteriously, he would turn into a better fielder and hitter. Now as he raced through the long grass his mind kept coming back to the evil thing that was wadded up in his pocket. He had to tell somebody about it or he would burst. He couldn't call the professor again. So then who . . .

As he jogged nearer to the mob of yelling, gesturing boys Johnny began to grin broadly. He waved excitedly. There was Fergie.

Fergie was sitting in the long grass, looking absolutely nonchalant as he chewed on a tufted weed. He was on the team that was up at bat. It was a chilly day, and so he was wearing an old scruffy gray sweat shirt with CYCLOPS ATHLETIC CLUB printed in white block letters across the front.

"Hi, Fergie," said Johnny, slumping down on the grass. Johnny tried hard to smile, but when he thought of the wadded paper in his pocket, his smile turned to a tense frown.

Fergie looked at Johnny curiously. "Hey, what's the matter with you? Did you bet on the Germans to win the Second World War?"

Normally Johnny would have laughed, but he was not in a very jokey mood. He dug his hand into his pants pocket and pulled out the piece of paper. Carefully he uncrumpled it, smoothed it out on his knee, and handed it to Fergie.

"I found this in the car when I went downtown with Mr. Brentlinger. I think it's a death threat."

Fergie squinted at the crumpled drawing and laughed. "A *death threat*? Are you out of your jug? This is one of those things from that book, whatsitsname, that the Pilgrims made so kids would learn their ABC's. I looked at it in the library once. This one's for the letter Y. What made you think it was a death threat?"

"Somebody left it on the seat where I was sitting in Mr. Brentlinger's car. Doncha see? They're after me on account of I know where the will is, and . . ." Johnny paused and stared at the ground. He bit his lip and felt his cheeks getting red with embarrassment. He had been running on because he was excited and scared, and he had not stopped to think that this would make absolutely no sense to Fergie. And now Fergie would probably decide that Johnny was weird. He would get up and walk away, and that would be the end of their friendship.

But that was not what happened. Fergie was staring at Johnny, but it was an interested stare. There was a gleam in his eyes and a faint curling smile on his lips. "He-ey," he said slowly, "are you mixed up in something? You can tell me, I won't rat on you. Come on."

So Johnny started to tell Fergie about Staunton Harold and the lost Glomus will and the table with the weird collection of objects on it. While they talked there was a lot of yelling and screaming going on behind their backs. Fergie's team was knocking the cover off the ball. Pretty soon the bases were loaded.

"Hey, Fergie!" somebody yelled. "You're up!"

"Oops. 'Scuse me! I'll be right back," said Fergie, and he scrambled to his feet. He picked up a bat and loped toward the plate. As Johnny watched, Fergie got ready to hit. The pitcher barreled the ball in, and Fergie swung. It was an awkward, lunging swing, and he missed. Johnny felt sympathetic and got ready to cheer Fergie up when he struck out. But then the ball came whizzing toward the plate again, and Fergie swung and connected. *Wok!* The ball sailed upward in a high, beautiful arc. It flew out over the head of the center fielder and came down in some bushes at the far end of the field. Fergie raced around the bases as all the boys on his team whooped and cheered. After he crossed home plate, Fergie stumbled back to where he'd been sitting before. He sat down, crossed his legs, and smiled modestly.

"Natural ability," he said, brushing an imaginary

speck of dust off his sweat shirt. "Okay, now. You wanna tell me some more about this trouble you're in?"

So Johnny told Fergie the rest of what he knew and what he guessed. He told him that he thought the lost Glomus will must be out at the estate called Staunton Harold. Fergie listened to all this thoughtfully. He nodded sometimes or shook his head, and now and then he would say something like "Hot dog! How about that!" or "Boy, that old guy must really have been out of his jug!" "Out of his jug" was one of Fergie's favorite expressions.

Finally Johnny was finished. He folded his arms and glanced nervously at Fergie. "Whaddaya think?" he asked.

Fergie was quiet a second before answering. "I think you're the only kid I know who's ever had a death threat handed to him. Honest! I never heard of it happening before!"

Johnny felt confused and kind of angry. First Fergie had said that the picture wasn't a death threat, and now he said that it was. Was he trying to be funny? "It's not like the Congressional Medal of Honor," he snapped back. "I mean, I might get killed."

"Yeah, you might." Fergie said this in an abstracted, dreamy way. It was plain that his mind was elsewhere. As Johnny stared at him anxiously Fergie hummed and gazed off into space. Suddenly a light came into his eyes. He snapped his fingers and turned to Johnny. "Hey!" he said. "You know what we oughta do?"

"What?"

"We oughta sneak out of our rooms tonight and go see if we can find a way to get into that Statler Harrison place. Whaddaya say?"

"It's Staunton Harold," said Johnny severely. He hated to hear people mispronounce names.

"Statler Hilton, Staunton Harold, what's the difference?" said Fergie with an irritated shrug. "Come on, answer the question. Do you wanta go or don't you?"

Johnny hemmed and hawed. He had a holy terror of violating rules and regulations, and camp regulations said that you couldn't leave your dormitory between lights-out and reveille. "We can't go," said Johnny fretfully. "If we get caught, they'll throw us out, and my grampa and gramma'll really feel awful if that happens."

Fergie snorted disgustedly. "Oh, come on, Dixon! Are you gonna spend the rest of your life wrapped up in a blanket in your bedroom? The only way to have any fun is to break the rules sometimes! Come on! I'll meet you at eleven P.M. out by the flagpole. There's a path over there," Fergie said, pointing off toward a mass of bushes near the tennis courts, "and it leads out toward that road. You know, the one we were hikin' on when we saw the old place. We'll just go out an' peek at the old dump an' come right back. Who's to know? You'll be in bed before anybody knows you left. Whaddaya say?"

Johnny still looked hesitant. "Eckelbecker'll turn me in if he finds out I've gone out."

Fergie looked grim. "You tell that lard bucket that

Byron Q. Ferguson told him to keep his trap shut unless he wants to have his ears tied into a bowknot behind his head."

Johnny was torn with indecision. The professor was always telling him that he ought to be more adventurous. Maybe he ought to quit worrying and live a little. "Oh, okay!" he said finally. "I'll be there."

At about five past eleven that night Johnny was standing out by the flagpole, waiting. It was a chilly, raw night with a fine mist in the air, and he was shivering as he peered up at the overcast sky. He was wearing his Notre Dame warm-up jacket over his pajama tops, and he also had on his blue jeans and his heavy socks and tennis shoes. He looked off toward the log buildings. So where was Fergie? Had he chickened out in spite of all his brave talk? But then Johnny saw a shape moving toward him. Fergie was sprinting across the wet grass, carrying something in his hand. Suddenly Johnny realized what it was—a flashlight. And then he felt very stupid: he had a flashlight, but it was in his suitcase. He had been so nervous and flustered about this whole deal that he had forgotten to bring it.

Fergie arrived, panting. "Hi!" he whispered. "Glad you didn't cop out on me. You bring a flashlight?"

"I don't have one," said Johnny untruthfully. "Is . . . is that all right?"

"Naw," said Fergie, grinning. "You get three demerits an' no supper tonight. Sure it's all right! Stop bein' such a fussbudget! This flashlight here is one of those super-duper sealed-beam jobbies. It shines for miles. So don't worry. Let's get started."

Fergie and Johnny jogged off into the drizzly darkness. After a couple of minutes Fergie switched on the wonderful sealed-beam flashlight. The effect was quite dramatic: A long bar of pale light shot out into the gloom. As Johnny watched, Fergie moved the beam back and forth. It lit up the hump of the pitcher's mound on the baseball diamond, and then it moved slowly across the mass of bushes beyond the field. The beam picked out a cleft in the wall of shrubbery.

"Aha!" said Fergie. "Aha, and other expressions of delight! Come on! We've got it knocked!"

The two boys marched on. They reached the edge of the wide grassy field and plunged into the gap in the bushes. It was a narrow path, and they had to go single file. Fergie went first with the light. Wet leaves slapped across Johnny's face, and he put out his arm to fend them off. His head was sopping wet now, and water was running down his neck. He thought about his gramma, and how she believed that if you got wet out in the rain, you might die of pneumonia. Poor Gramma! Johnny hoped that she was really going to get better. Silently he said a Hail Mary and an Our Father for her.

After what seemed like hours of slopping along through wet underbrush, the boys came out onto a road covered with wet gravel. Johnny had a vague idea that they were walking through a forest, but when he looked up, he couldn't tell where the trees ended and the sky began. Fergie's light slashed out through the mist like a sword. Neither boy spoke.

Johnny began to brood about the mysterious place that they had set out to explore. The old mansion was evil-looking, even in bright sunlight. What would it be like at night?

Fergie grabbed Johnny's arm. "Hey! What was that?" he said sharply, and he sounded alarmed.

Both boys halted and stood dead-still, listening. Off to their left they heard noises. *Crunch, crunch, crackle, crunch.* Somebody—or something—was thrashing through the wet underbrush. Johnny wanted to run. But he had his pride; if Fergie was going to stand his ground, then so would he.

"Hey! What the heck d'ya think *that* was?" Fergie was trying to sound brave, but Johnny could hear the trembling in his voice.

"I dunno. Maybe it was a dog."

"Naw. Too much noise for a dog. I'd say it was a hunter, only any hunter who was out here on a lousy night like this would have to be out of his jug. Some old bum maybe."

Johnny didn't think it was a bum. In his mind's eye he saw a Frankensteinish creature dripping green slime from its horny paws. Any minute now it would come charging out of the darkness at them, uttering strange cries and lusting for their blood.

Suddenly the noise in the underbrush died away. Fergie took a deep breath and let it out.

"Hot dog!" he said, grinning. "He must've gone away." Fergie chuckled. His old jaunty, swaggering self was coming back. "Let's move it! It's just a little ways down the road to the old place."

On the boys hiked while the wet gravel went *squrch, squrch* under their feet. The mist turned into a steady drizzle. Johnny kept straining to see, but he could not make out much except more road and vague leafy shadows crowding in close on either side. Finally, though, as they started down a hill, the close shadows of trees and bushes fell away. The long beam of Fergie's flashlight swerved to the left and picked out the heavily ornamented stone arch, with its swags and urns and columns. They were there. They had reached Staunton Harold.

And standing under the arch, waiting for them, was a man. He wore a yellow rubber raincoat and a black rubber rain hat with a wide floppy brim. Under his armpit the man held a flashlight, and in his hands was a rifle—pointed straight at Johnny and Fergie.

CHAPTER SEVEN

❧•❧

The drizzling rain kept falling. The still beam of Fergie's flashlight shone straight at the menacing figure's face. Even with the brim of the rain hat partially hiding the face, Johnny knew who it was immediately. It was the young man with the bug eyes and receding chin who had glared at him in the lobby of the Squam House.

Shifting the gun in his hands, the man took a step forward. "Okay, you two," he said nastily. "Just you hold it, right there! Now, would you mind tellin' me what you're supposed to be doin'? Huh?"

Johnny was terrified. He had a sudden vision of himself and Fergie lying by the roadside, shot full of holes and covered with blood.

Fergie, however, was made of sterner stuff. He stepped forward and challenged the man angrily. "Hey, you, what do you mean pointin' that gun at us? This's a public road. We ain't done nothin' wrong!"

The man looked at Fergie thoughtfully for a second. He looked down at the rifle in his hand. And then, amazingly, his whole attitude changed. "*Darnit!*" he yelled disgustedly, and he threw the rifle down on the ground. "Darnit all anyway!" He tore off his rain hat and threw it into a mud puddle. Then he sat down on a piece of carved stone that stood in the grass near the arch. "Go ahead!" he said, wringing his hands and staring gloomily at the ground. "Do what you want! Steal my gun! Break into the house! Make fun of me! See if I care! I try to be tough, but I just can't do it!"

Johnny and Fergie were totally stunned by this dramatic turnaround. They looked at each other, and then Fergie stepped forward.

"We don't want your dumb gun," he said. "And we're not gonna break into anybody's house. We just don't like to have people threatening us." Fergie pointed off into the darkness. "That house over there—is it yours?"

The young man nodded glumly. "Sort of. It belongs to my family. My name is Chadwick Glomus, and my grandfather was good old H. Bagwell Glomus. Or Grampa Herbie, as he was known in the family. I have too much money, and a lot of time on my hands, so every now and then I come up to this old place and look for Grampa Herbie's will."

Johnny was astonished. He had figured that he was the only one in the world who knew that the puzzle in Mr. Glomus's office pointed toward this place. Without pausing to think, he said excitedly, "Hey! How'd you guess that—"

The young man gave him a sour glance. "Oh, I'm clever. Very clever. And I gather you worked out that part of the riddle too. When I saw you at the hotel, I figured that you had come up here to search for the will. You see, I was working in the gift shop the day you visited my dear grandfather's cereal factory. You were babbling a blue streak about the puzzle to that old man you were with, and so I figured you might be on to something."

Johnny gasped. So that was it. He *had* seen the man before!

The young man smiled unpleasantly. "I hope you find the will, and I hope it turns out that everybody in the Glomus family has been cut out of it. I hope that Grampa Herbie left his dough to the Christian Scientists or the Red Sox or a home for retired organ-grinders! I hope nobody in my family gets a red cent!"

Fergie looked at the young man strangely. "Why don't you like your family? What's the matter with them?"

The young man put his hand over his face. "Oh, don't ask! Don't ask! But if you really want to know, the main reason why everybody is such a mess is Grampa Herbie. He was one of the most awful people you'd ever want to meet in your life! Always harping on the importance of a balanced diet. Chew your food thirty-two times before you swallow it! Did you know that a bowl of Oaty Crisps contains ninety-three percent of your recommended daily allowance of iron, riboflavin, and niacin? *Yaargh!* And then, at the end of his life, to start messing around with black magic the way he did! And to top it all off, that insane puzzle about the will!"

The young man shook his head and winced. "Ow! I wish you hadn't gotten me started on my family. I think it's giving me a headache!"

Agin Johnny and Fergie glanced at each other. They both felt sorry for the young man, but right now they wanted to go back to camp. They had decided that their adventure had reached a dead end, and they needed some nice, polite way of saying good-bye.

"Uh, we . . . we better be gettin' back to our camp," said Fergie, with a nervous glance over his shoulder. "If the counselors find out we're not in bed, they'll really blow their tops."

The young man looked very unhappy. At first he had seemed threatening, but now he merely seemed strange, wistful, and more than a little bit lonely.

"Oh, please don't go yet!" he pleaded. "I'm sorry I pointed that gun at you! Look, if you stay just a bit, I'll show you something."

Fergie wrinkled up his nose suspiciously. "Yeah? What?"

"It's a secret passage that runs under the fence and comes up inside the chapel next to the big house. The tunnel is a big Glomus family secret, but I'll let you in on it."

Johnny felt very nervous about this. He had always had it drummed into his head, ever since he was little, that you never went anywhere with strangers. And this was a stranger who was stranger than most.

The young man looked at Fergie and Johnny, and read their thoughts. With a pained expression on his face he got up and fished his rain hat out of the mud puddle. He shook it a few times and jammed it back onto his head. "Please believe me!" he said in a pleading, sad voice. "I'm not a murderer! I can't even shoot squirrels! That gun is empty. See for yourselves!"

Fergie took a few steps forward and picked up the gun. He slid the bolt back and pointed the beam of his flashlight in the chamber. Then he slammed the bolt back into place and handed it to the young man. "Yeah, you're right," he said, nodding. "Okay, look. I'll level with you. We were just gonna peer through the fence at that old dump over there and then hightail it back to camp. But if you wanna show us somethin', we could stay for, oh, maybe about half an hour." Fergie paused and turned to look back at Johnny, who was just standing there fidgeting. "That okay with you, John baby?"

Johnny glanced fretfully over his shoulder. He had mixed emotions. He was afraid of getting caught if he stayed out too late, but the idea of a secret passage really excited him. It was the kind of thing he had always dreamed of finding.

"I guess we could stay for a little while," he said hesitantly.

And so it was settled. The young man turned and walked back toward the stone arch, motioning for the other two to follow him. They headed along a narrow muddy path that ran down a little slope and off into the woods. As they tramped along, Johnny found that he was getting really nervous, but he was also getting really interested. He wondered what the passage would be like.

On they marched, over masses of soggy leaves, while water dripped all around them. Finally they came to a small clearing where Johnny could see the dark shadow of a small building. It seemed to be a funny little cottage of some kind. Fergie swept his flashlight beam upward, and Johnny saw part of a slate roof, a brick wall, and a little window with diamond-shaped panes. A door was set in a fancy stone arch. Over the arch was a stone banner with the inscription *Health Is Wealth*.

"This is one of those cute little outbuildings or lodges that you find around big estates sometimes," said the young man as he fumbled in his pocket for a key. He turned it in the lock and gave the door a good hard shove. Then he disappeared inside. Johnny and Fergie hesitated for a second and then followed him into a musty-smelling room with no furniture in it. Built into one wall was a very fancy marble fireplace. It was covered with stone knobs carved to look like the tiny heads of children. They were smiling and apple-cheeked, and were slurping cereal from bowls. Over the mantel was a mildewed oil painting of good old Mr. Glomus himself, with a box of Oaty Crisps in his hands.

The young man laid his rifle on the mantel. Then he grabbed one of the carved heads and twisted it. Johnny heard the clanking and clattering of hidden weights and chains. And then, as the young man pointed the beam of his flashlight into the dark mouth of the fireplace, Johnny saw the back wall of the hearth slide up. A low opening was revealed, with steps leading down.

The young man folded his arms and stared calmly down into the dark opening, laughing harshly. "Good old Grampa Herbie really thought of everything! If you're out shooting quail and a thunderstorm hits, you duck in here. And then you can scoot right over, zippity-zoo, to the chapel without getting your head wet. And now, if you've got a few minutes more, I'll show you part of the passage."

But before starting out, the young man did a strange thing. He stepped back, reached up onto the mantel, and took down a candle and a book of matches. Then he poked around in the darkness for a few minutes and came up with a long knobby bronze candlestick. Humming tunelessly, he screwed the candle into the holder and lit it.

"Whaddaya need that for?" asked Fergie. "You've got a flashlight, doncha? Or did your batteries run out?"

"The batteries are Everready batteries and will last for centuries," said the young man dryly. "This is for something else." His face suddenly grew grim and hard. In the candlelight it looked like the face of a gaunt and cadaverous ghost. "Have you two heard about the Guardian?"

Johnny stared. This was something new to him, and to Fergie too.

"Don't know, eh?" said the young man tauntingly. "Well, kiddies, the Guardian is something my irresponsible grandfather whipped up when he was fooling around with the black arts. He called it up out of the depths, out of the void, and it's still here, wandering around this old estate. The Guardian can be anything: It might be a pool of moonlight on the floor, or a chair, or smoke drifting in the air. And if it catches you . . . well, one of my great-uncles was caught by it. Afterward they buried him in a hurry." The young man paused and grinned unpleasantly. "Do you know what a mummy looks like after it's been unwrapped? Just a dried brown husk that used to be a human being, with holes for eyes? Well, that's what Great-Uncle Platt looked like after the Guardian got him. And I'll tell you something else you may not know. Three people have disappeared in this area in the last five years. No bodies were ever found, but I'll bet you—dollars to doughnuts—that the Guardian got them too."

Fergie's eyebrows went up. He was pretty suspicious about all this. "So, if there's this monster down there," he said, "why are we goin' on down to meet it? Is it monster-feeding time or what?"

The young man stared stonily at Fergie. "You can make fun all you want, my friend," he said grumpily. "But what I'm telling you happens to be true! And in answer to your question, the Guardian isn't there all the time. But I suspect that it will come for you if you get too close to the will. I have this candle. If an evil presence is near, candle flames burn blue. That's what Shakespeare says, and it happens to be the truth. So come along. . . ."

Fergie and Johnny looked at each other. Neither of them believed a word the young man was saying.

"Yeah, sure, let's go," said Fergie, with a jaunty leer and a devil-may-care shrug of his shoulders. "If you don't mind about monsters, neither do we."

The young man smiled a crooked, mocking smile. With the candlestick in one hand and a flashlight in the other, he bent over and stepped down into the narrow opening. Fergie went next, and Johnny came last. Down a dark, damp-smelling staircase passage they went. Johnny counted twenty-three steps to the bottom. Then the floor leveled off, and the passage grew wider. They were in a stone tunnel where three people could walk abreast. Fergie flashed his light around, and Johnny saw, at the top of an arch they were passing under, a smiling stone cherub and the carved motto *Mens sana in sano corpore*, which means "a sound mind in a sound body." Over by one wall of the tunnel some junk was piled up.

"Charming place, isn't it?" said the young man as they walked along. "I understand Grampa Herbie originally wanted to make this a little subway line, with a pneumatic-powered car and all. But he lost interest when he found out how much it would cost."

They walked on. In places there was a strong smell of earth, and Johnny noticed that pieces of the ceiling had caved in. Sometimes the walls were slick with damp, and here and there Johnny saw streaks of yellowish-green niter oozing down over carved corbels and columns. Every now and then he glanced at the flame of the candle that the young man was carrying. It burned sluggishly, because the air in this underground place was rather stale. But it did not burn blue.

Finally they stopped. Before them was a nail-studded wooden door set in a stone arch with a zigzag molding around it.

"End of the line," said the young man with a little sigh. He turned to face the two boys. "This door leads to the crypt under the chapel next to the big ghastly old house. You two must have seen it from the road. But I don't think we ought to go upstairs. No, I wouldn't want to take the responsibility if anything happened to you two. Let's head back."

Johnny was disappointed. He had not believed any of the young man's warnings about the Guardian and he wanted to see the inside of the spooky old chapel. Also he had a funny idea that was lodged firmly in his head:

If he could only get onto the grounds of the estate, he would be able to figure out the rest of the Glomus puzzle.

Fergie protested and Johnny wheedled, but the young man was quite firm. So, back they went and up the narrow stairs into the dusty little room where the journey had started. The young man blew out his candle and set it on the mantelpiece. He twisted the carved knob, and the stone slab at the back of the hearth came bumping and grumbling back down. Then, taking the rifle again and tucking it under his arm, he led the boys out of the lodge, locked the door, and slid the key into a hole in one of the carved ball-flowers over the door. And now the three of them were tramping back along the muddy path through the trees.

When they reached the gravel road, the young man stopped again. "Gentlemen, I am going to take my leave," he said, bowing stiffly. "My car is parked not far from here, and I gather you two can make it back to camp all right. I'm so glad I had a chance to entertain you. And if you ever think of me, remember that there are things in this world that are better than having lots of money. Like having all your marbles, which I don't seem to. Good day. It's really been, as they say."

And with that the young man wheeled abruptly and marched off down the road.

"Weird," said Fergie, shaking his head. "Weird is the word for that character."

"Yeah, but he was kind of nice, anyway," said Johnny thoughtfully.

"Uh-huh," grunted Fergie, and he screwed his mouth up into a distrustful frown. Then the two explorers turned and began walking quickly back toward camp. For a few minutes the only sound was the pattering of rain and the crunching of gravel under the soles of their shoes. Then suddenly the air was split by long, loud, hideous yells and shrieks.

Johnny and Fergie stopped dead in their tracks. The yelling had come from the stretch of road that the young man had just been heading for. The two boys did not discuss what they ought to do. Instead, they turned around and set off running, pell-mell, in the direction they had come from. Johnny was not a great runner, but he ran hard, determined not to be left behind in the dark. Suddenly the two of them stopped, breathless, in the middle of the road. The jumping, bouncing beam of Fergie's flashlight had picked out something. On the rain-soaked gravel lay two objects: One was a rifle, and the other was a flashlight. The flashlight was still on, and it cast its long, narrow beam out across the gravel of the road. On the handle was a raised oval medallion that bore the gold initials CG.

CHAPTER EIGHT

Horrified, Johnny looked at Fergie. Fergie was staring down at the rifle and the flashlight, still breathing hard from the long run. Abruptly he stopped to pick up the flashlight. He flipped it over to Johnny, who was so surprised that he almost dropped it.

"Here," said Fergie. "Now we've each got one. Come on. Let's get headed back to camp."

Johnny was flabbergasted. He stood there opening and shutting his mouth. Finally he managed to speak. "You mean . . . you mean you're gonna just . . . just . . ."

Fergie hesitated. For a second he stared off into the darkness, and there was fear in his eyes. Then he laughed harshly. His lips curled into a cynical and knowing smile. "Yeah," he said, "we're gonna *just*. We're gonna mosey on back and get some sleepy-bye, if we can. Look, John baby, don't you see what happened? He dropped his stuff here in the road. Then he yelled bloody murder for a coupla minutes, an' then he lit out into the woods. He's probably out there right now, laughin' at us. You didn't *believe* all that junk about a monster that turns people into mummies, did you?"

Johnny was silent. Up until now he had not believed the strange young man's stories, but he was beginning to have second thoughts. Johnny looked down at the chrome-plated flashlight he held in his hands. It looked expensive. And there was the rifle lying there too. "Maybe you're right," he said slowly, "but . . . well, would he really have left this stuff just layin' here?"

Fergie shrugged. "Why not? He's rich as Croesus, so he can buy himself more rifles and flashlights, can't he? Besides, he's got a screw loose. Crazy people do crazy things."

Again Johnny was silent. It seemed to him that Fergie was being very reasonable and logical. All the same, he had his doubts. Finally, with a weary shrug, he said "Oh, okay! Let's go on back."

"Right," said Fergie, nodding. Then, on a sudden impulse, he tucked his flashlight under his armpit and cupped his hands to his mouth. "NIGHTY-NIGHT, CHAD BABY!" he yelled. There was no answer. But then, the boys didn't expect one.

Fergie and Johnny did not try to take the rifle back

with them. They left it lying on the rain-soaked road and slogged on back to camp. At the flagpole they parted, and each one ran back to his own building. As he slipped in, closing the door softly behind him, Johnny noticed the clock in the downstairs hall. It said five minutes before two.

Johnny didn't get much sleep that night. He was still terribly keyed up, and he lay tossing and turning for a long time, until—around five A.M.—he dozed off, and had a dream about Mr. Glomus chasing him through an endless tunnel. And then, before he knew it, reveille was blowing again, and Johnny crawled out of bed to face another day.

When he came stumbling into the dining hall for breakfast, Johnny felt like one of the walking dead. For two straight nights he had gone without much sleep, and now it was beginning to get to him. He shuffled along the cafeteria line, sliding his tray over the stainless-steel bars. As he was staring blearily at the bins of scrambled eggs, he heard the women behind the counter talking to each other.

"Hey, Edna!" said one, "didja hear that thing on the radio? About the guy that got lost last night?"

"No, I didn't. So what happened?"

"Well, it was the same like all o' the others. He just disappeared! They found his gun layin' in the road out near that old mansion—you know the one I mean. An' then they found his car parked up the road, with the keys in it. I betcha they never find him! Remember old Mrs. Spofford an' Charley Holmes an' that bum—what was his name, anyway? They never found none of 'em! An' I bet they never will, either!"

Johnny was wide awake now. He stared so hard at the woman who was telling the story that she noticed him and suddenly clammed up. "Milk or Kool-Aid?" she asked in a toneless voice as she shoved a plate of scrambled eggs and bacon at Johnny.

Mechanically Johnny took a glass of milk and moved on down the line with his tray. His brain was racing madly. So it hadn't been just a tall tale. Chad really had disappeared, and there were others who had gone before him. Distractedly Johnny looked this way and that. Ah, there was Fergie waving and motioning for him to come and sit down.

Scuttling sideways, Johnny made his way down the narrow aisle between two rows of tables. He put his tray down, climbed onto a seat, and immediately began talking.

"Guess what!" he said breathlessly, "I just listened to those two women up there at the counter, and they claim that that guy we met really *has* disappeared! And there's others who've been missing too!"

Fergie looked at Johnny scornfully. "Aw, come on, Dixon! Those two old bags'd believe anything they heard."

"You . . . you mean you don't think—"

Fergie laughed and shook his head vigorously. "Naah,

I *don't* think! Really, Dixon, you're one of the most superstitious kids I ever met in my life! Look. That guy was a crazy, right? He was playin' a joke, an' then maybe he screwed up an' he really *did* get lost. An' you wanna know what else I think? I think he's the one that left that weird picture in the car for you. It'd be just like him. He's really out of his jug! So don't worry about him—he'll turn up, one way or the other."

"Uh-huh," said Johnny weakly. He was not convinced by what Fergie had said, but he didn't feel like arguing. He remembered the awful, agonized screams they had heard. Johnny felt sorry for Chad. He really had kind of liked him. And then, suddenly, it occurred to him that they shouldn't be talking about last night's escapade at all. What if some creepy kid like Eckelbecker heard them and turned them in? Anxiously Johnny shot a glance at the kid who was sitting across the table. But he did not seem to be paying any attention to Johnny and Fergie. His eyes were on his plate, and he was busy stuffing scrambled eggs into his mouth.

Fergie elbowed Johnny in the side. "Don't worry about him," he said, snickering. "His ears are fulla strawberry jam."

At this, however, Eckelbecker did look up.

Days passed. Johnny learned Indian lore and made a belt out of little interlocking pieces of leather. With the other boys he hiked for miles and miles, and on Saturday he got to climb Mount Chocorua. It was a long, exhausting climb, and near the top it got scary because the path skirted the edge of a drop-off. But Johnny made it to the top like everyone else, and it gave him a great sense of accomplishment. He had done something courageous and difficult that he wouldn't have been able to do a week or a month ago.

At the last fireside folk sing on Saturday night Johnny stood proudly with the other Scouts as they sang:

> Softly falls the light of day
> As our campfire fades away
> Silently each Scout should ask
> Have I done my daily task?
> Have I kept my honor bright?
> Can I guiltless rest tonight?
> Have I done and have I dared
> Everything to Be Prepared?

Johnny felt the warmth of the fire on his face, and he felt friendly toward the other boys around him. He was sad about leaving, but he would be glad to see Gramma and find out how she was doing. Then he thought about Chad Glomus. He had never been found. For days search parties had been combing the wooded areas around Mount Chocorua, but he had not turned up. Johnny wondered if he should come forward and tell about what he and Fergie had seen. But to do that, Johnny would have had to admit that he had been out in the woods running around after taps. And he was scared of getting into trouble.

And there was something else on Johnny's mind too. It was the whole business of the Glomus will and the baffling collection of clues on the table. Johnny was absolutely convinced that he had figured out the first part of the puzzle, that the will was out at the estate called Staunton Harold. But beyond that point he was stuck. And come Sunday he was going to be even more stuck because he'd be back in Duston Heights and the secret hiding place of the Glomus will would be far, far away from him. Even if he ever solved the riddle of the sign from the tea shop, he would probably never get a chance to test his theories—or collect that lovely ten thousand dollar reward.

Sunday arrived, and Johnny packed up his things, shook hands with Mr. Brentlinger, and said good-bye. Then he climbed aboard the big black-and-yellow bus with all the other Scouts. He was really sorry that he had to go, and as the bus pulled away from camp there were tears in Johnny's eyes.

But on the ride back, he had a good time. He got a seat with Fergie, and the two of them really talked up a storm. For the first time Johnny discovered that Fergie lived in Duston Heights! The two of them had never met because Fergie lived over on the other side of town, and he went to public school. Johnny wondered at first why Fergie had been so closemouthed about where he lived, but it gradually dawned on him that Fergie was poor. He and his family lived on the third floor of a triple-decker apartment house down near the railroad tracks, and Fergie's father sold mail-order shoes and encyclopedias for a living.

Around three o'clock in the afternoon the bus pulled into the parking lot next to the town hall in Duston Heights. When Johnny got out, he had his pack and his sleeping bag strapped on his back and his cardboard suitcase in his hand. He looked this way and that, and then he saw the professor and Grampa standing next to the professor's old mud-spattered Ford. Although Grampa was wearing his usual gray shirt and gray wash pants, the professor was all done up in his blue pinstripe suit, with the vest and the Phi Beta Kappa key that dangled from his gold watch chain. They were both smiling and waving at Johnny, but as he waved back it suddenly struck him that their smiles were forced. There was something in their eyes that said *Johnny, we have bad news for you*. With fear clutching at his heart, Johnny wondered if the bad news had something to do with Gramma.

CHAPTER NINE

❧•❧

Johnny shook hands with the professor and Grampa. He introduced Fergie, who plunged into the milling crowd of relatives and Scouts and came back dragging his dad. Mr. Ferguson turned out to be a mild little man with glasses and thinning hair. He said hello and then headed off with Fergie in the direction of their car. There was an awkward silence until the professor coughed and said brusquely that it was time to be heading back.

Johnny stowed his luggage in the trunk of the car. He climbed into the front with the professor, Grampa climbed into the back, and off they went. Except for the hum of the motor there was absolute silence. To Johnny this was maddening. He wanted to yell, *What is it? What's the matter?*, but his fear and his usual timidity forced him to keep his mouth shut. Finally they arrived at 28 Fillmore Street.

The professor pulled up with a jolt and a sudden screech of the brakes. There, standing on the steps with a big smile on her face, was Gramma! Johnny was amazed, and he felt very relieved. The way Grampa and the professor had been acting, he had expected to find a wreath with a black ribbon on the door and Gramma laid out in a coffin in the living room. But, no, there she was, leaning on a cane with a funny white stocking cap on her head. Her eyes were bright, and she seemed very cheerful. Johnny let out a wild shriek of delight, ran up the walk, and threw his arms around her.

"Gramma!" he yelled. "You're okay! Hooray!"

"Well, I'm sorta okay," said Gramma, frowning. "Your grandfather is gonna scold me for comin' out here. But I didn't wanta be lollin' around in the parlor like some kinda *invalid*."

Soon Grampa and the professor were at Gramma's side. They were clucking like a couple of elderly hens, telling her that she was supposed to be inside lying down. Somehow, with a lot of door-slamming and shuffling around, everybody got back inside the house. Grampa helped Gramma into the parlor and got her seated in the big bristly brown easy chair. Then the professor went out to the kitchen and started fixing Sunday dinner. The professor could cook, which was a good thing—Johnny didn't know if he could take another of Grampa's ghastly meals. Every now and then Johnny would glance at Grampa and see the same secretive look he had noticed before. What were they hiding from him?

Eventually dinner was served in the dining room. With Grampa's help Gramma hobbled out to join them. It was a good meal—shepherd's pie, a dish the professor had learned to make when he was in England, and ice cream sundaes for dessert. But halfway through dinner Gramma got drowsy and started to complain of a headache. So Grampa helped her into the back bedroom, made her comfortable, and came back to finish his meal.

After dinner the professor asked Johnny to join him and Grampa in the parlor. *Uh oh*, thought Johnny, *here comes the bad news.*

The professor sat down on the sofa. He rubbed his hands nervously and looked solemn. "John," he began, in a tight, strained voice, "there is a passage in Shakespeare that goes, *When troubles come, they come not single spies, but in battalions.* And that has certainly been the case lately around here. Your grandmother's trouble is over with—at least, we hope it is. But on Thursday your grandfather got a telegram from the Department of Defense. And it was bad news. Your father's plane was shot down over North Korea, in enemy territory."

There was a heavy silence in the room. Johnny felt a

tightening in his chest. With an effort he forced himself to speak. "Is . . . is he . . ."

The professor sighed wearily. "We don't know. There's no word one way or the other. He was a good pilot, with good reflexes. I think there's reason to believe that he could have parachuted to safety, in which case he is probably a prisoner now, or will be soon. But as bad as that is, it's better, far better than . . . the alternative."

"It sure is," said Grampa, nodding. He patted Johnny on the back and smiled sadly at him. "Don't you worry, John. Your dad'll be okay. I read in the paper the other day about how a pilot who got shot down stole a rowboat an' rowed all the way to Japan an' got rescued. Don't you worry—he'll be back soon."

Yeah, thought Johnny gloomily. *He will if he's still alive.* He thought about Chad Glomus, who either was or was not alive. And then he thought about all the stories he had ever read about missing persons. There was the famous Judge Crater, who had gone out to dinner one evening and had never come back. There was Amelia Earhart, the aviator who had disappeared in her plane. Would his dad become a missing person like that? Would Johnny be waiting twenty or thirty years from now for some news of the great Korean War pilot who had vanished without a trace? Black despair filled his heart. He had been so happy about coming home. He had planned to tell Grampa and the professor about his mysterious midnight meeting with Chad Glomus and about the secret passage and everything. But now he didn't want to talk about anything.

The late-afternoon sunlight fell slanting through the parlor windows. It was a nice day outside—for some people.

Finally the professor spoke. He was not much good at comforting other people because he was such a prickly, snappish person, but he tried. "Well, John," he said, "all we can do is hope and pray. There's no reason to despair until there are definite *reasons* for despair."

The professor was being logical, but logic wasn't going to help Johnny much right now. It took a real effort to shove himself to his feet and go upstairs to work on the Latin homework assignment that Sister Mary Anthony had given the class to do during the week's vacation. He opened his Latin book, heaved a great sigh, and soon he was busy with *fruor* and *ulciscor* and *fungor* and lots of other lovely deponent verbs. But over and over as he turned the pages of his book he saw in his mind's eye his father's jet plane bursting into a bright bloom of fire.

October passed. The loud winds of autumn stripped the leaves from the trees on Fillmore Street. Johnny helped his grandfather rake the leaves into a pile in the driveway, and then they had a bonfire, and Johnny threw chestnuts into the fire to make them pop. Gramma got steadily better every day, and soon she was up and about—against the doctor's advice. On school days Johnny went back and forth between his home and St. Michael's School. Some days after school he would go down to Peter's Sweet Shop, a soda fountain on Merrimack Street, and talk with Fergie, and gobble various gooey concoctions. And often in the evening Fergie would come over to Johnny's house to play chess or have weird-fact contests or just sit around and blab. At six P.M. every day Johnny would turn on the television set and listen to the *CBS Evening News*. He kept hoping that he would hear some news about a jet pilot named Harrison Dixon or see a picture of his dad being turned loose by the North Koreans. But the Korean War raged on, and the newscasters said nothing about any prisoners being released. "No news is good news," said the professor, meaning that at least they hadn't heard that Johnny's dad was dead. But this bit of "comfort" did not help Johnny, and day by day, bit by bit, his gloom and pessimism deepened.

Ever since his mother had died of cancer, Johnny had been gnawed by the fear that he would be abandoned, that he would be left alone. To Johnny this now seemed like more than a possibility—it seemed terribly likely. His mother was dead, and his dad was missing in action; his grandmother had been terribly ill, and her illness might return. And then, if Gramma died, Grampa might get so gloomy that he wouldn't want to go on living. Then he would die, and Johnny would be left alone. There was the professor, of course, but Johnny was sure he wouldn't want to adopt him. Hadn't he heard the professor say, many times, that he enjoyed living alone? No. There would be no help there. If everybody close to him died, Johnny would be alone.

Johnny let this fear of abandonment grow. He worried about his father a lot, and he was always glancing anxiously at his gramma to see if she was all right. And now, strangely enough, Johnny's brooding about his grandmother's health brought him back to the lost Glomus will. His reasoning was that if Gramma got sick again, it would take a great brain surgeon to save her. They'd need money to pay one, but now that they had cashed in their savings bonds to pay for her first operation, they were next door to broke. All they had left was a small nest egg, something in a savings account, and something more in that tin can in their kitchen. Johnny didn't know how much great brain surgeons charged for their services, but he figured that it must be a lot. If only he could get the ten thousand dollar reward for finding the Glomus will, he would hire the best surgeon there was to operate on Gramma if her sickness came back.

This "reasoning" of Johnny's was a daydream, but it helped him handle his deep, dark fears. The Glomus will would save him when all else failed, and soon Johnny became obsessed with it. He thought about it all the time, and he became strangely secretive. He never did tell Grampa or the professor about his strange midnight meeting with Chad Glomus. Nor did he tell Grampa about his "Staunton Harold" theory, his guess about where the will was hidden. He wanted very much to discuss his theory with Fergie, but something made him hold back. He was afraid that Fergie might accidentally tell the professor or Grampa and that the two of them would get worried and try to stop him from going after the will. If he was going to save Gramma, he would have to be allowed to work out the puzzle and then do whatever was necessary after that. Until he was ready to make his move, Johnny figured that he'd better stay clammed up.

Often in the evening Johnny went to the public library to find out what he could about the Glomus family and their estate up in the White Mountains. He didn't find much, except for a little about Chad's disappearance in the back issues of *The Boston Globe*. He also managed to locate an article about the Staunton Harold estate in an old picture book called *Stately Homes of New England*. There were a few murky engravings, and there was the surprising information that Mr. Glomus was buried in a mausoleum on the grounds of the estate. All this was very interesting, but it did not throw any light on what the YE OLDE TEA SHOPPE sign meant. Sadly Johnny had to admit that he was up against a blank wall. He had tracked the will as far as the estate, but unless he were Superman, with X-ray vision, he didn't see how he was ever going to discover where it was hidden.

One cold, dark day early in November Johnny came home from school to find that nobody was there. Under the sugar bowl on the dining room table was a note, and it said,

> Dear Johnny,
> Have gone to take your grandmother to the hospital. Nothing to worry about. Just a checkup. We'll be back by dinnertime.
>
> Grampa

As he read this Johnny felt his blood run cold. If he had been in a more reasonable frame of mind, he would have known that there was nothing strange about Gramma's going back to the hospital for a checkup. But now he was convinced that Gramma was dying. What on earth could he do?

Johnny sat very still on one of the dining room chairs. Some people yell and scream when they are upset, but Johnny always got very quiet, cold, and withdrawn. He stared at the picture of the Last Supper that hung over the sideboard. But the picture was just a blur to him. Instead, he saw Mount Chocorua and the crumbling stone arch that said Staunton Harold. He saw a train chugging northward up into the White Mountains. And now, slowly, as the Sessions clock ticked on the sideboard, a plan began to form in Johnny's fevered brain. He would go up to New Hampshire, to the estate called Staunton Harold. He would get a room at the hotel that the fussy old lady ran. What was its name? Oh, well, it didn't matter. He had some stationery with the hotel's name and phone number on it—it had been passed out to the Scouts so they could write letters home. Then he'd go out to the estate, and somehow, by hook or by crook, he would find the lost Glomus will, claim the reward, and use the money to get a brain surgeon for Gramma.

This was a crazy plan, and in one corner of his brain Johnny knew it. It was also dangerous, but, strangely enough, the danger attracted him. Even though Johnny was timid, the kind of kid who always looks six ways before crossing the street, every now and then he got the urge to do wild, untimid things. He was always longing to break free from his nervous, scaredy-cat side. *All right, then. He would go.* He wouldn't tell the professor and he wouldn't tell Fergie, either. Johnny wanted this to be his triumph, his alone. *Okay. Let's get organized.* What did he need?

The quiet, reasonable Sessions clock ticked on. The shadows in the dining room grew longer. Johnny sat like somebody who is under a spell. His eyes shone, and his mind was racing like a runaway steam engine, churning out a plan, a wonderful, improbable plan.

CHAPTER TEN

Later that same day, when Gramma and Grampa got back from the hospital, they told Johnny that the checkup had gone okay—everything was all right. Johnny did not believe them for a minute. He was convinced they were faking. And so, quietly and secretly, as the November days passed, Johnny got ready to put his plan into action. He went down to the railroad station and asked the station master about trains that ran up into the White Mountains. He found there was a Boston & Maine train that stopped in Kancamagus Center twice a day, early in the morning and then again late at night. The late train, which left Duston Heights at five P.M. was the one Johnny wanted. He could duck out of the house around four thirty, catch the train, and be far away before anyone knew that he was missing.

Then there was the matter of money. He would need to pay for the train ticket and for his hotel room. Although Johnny didn't have any money stashed away, he knew that his grandparents did. They'd lived through the Depression of the 1930's, when the banks had failed, and they'd never gotten over their distrust of banks. So they kept most of their savings on the top kitchen cupboard shelf, inside a red Prince Albert tobacco can. It wasn't much—about a hundred dollars in small bills. Johnny felt very bad about taking it, but he told himself that it was the only way. To keep Grampa from getting suspicious he decided to leave the money where it was until the day came when, suddenly, he would leave.

Johnny also replaced the batteries in his old beat-up flashlight and started picking out the clothes he would need. He'd want all his warm winter things, that was for sure—his parka, his stocking cap, his leather gloves, and his woolen muffler. New Hampshire could turn into a real icebox, and according to the weather reports, there had already been snow up in the northern counties. He wondered what the chapel and the old gloomy mansion would look like in the winter. With a little thrill and a little nervousness, he realized that he would soon be finding out.

And when was he leaving? For a while he himself wasn't sure, but then he decided on November 15 for no special reason. Since it was coming up soon, he stepped up his preparations. And through it all he hugged his secret tightly to him, like a miser with a bag of gold, terribly afraid that somebody would find out what he was up to and try to stop him.

On the morning of November 14 Johnny woke up and found that he had a cold. He felt feverish and achy, and his head was all stuffed up.

Johnny groaned. He wanted to be in top shape for the expedition. Should he postpone it, then? Wouldn't it be better to wait till he was really ready? He wavered and fussed all through breakfast, on his way to school, and during school too. The more he thought, the more convinced he became that he should wait till he was feeling better. But, on the other hand, Gramma could be dying. Time was important. At three thirty, when school let out, he had still not reached a decision.

On his way home Johnny stopped by the library. He wanted to look at that book that contained the article about the Glomus estate. He headed straight into the stacks, took the book down, went to a table, and opened it up. The first time Johnny had read it, the article hadn't really sunk in. But this time it made an unforgettable impression. Once again he read that the mansion was adorned with statues of the Nine Worthies, whoever they were. The chapel was a replica of a seventeenth-century English chapel built by an English nobleman named Sir Robert Shirley. His estate was called Staunton Harold, which was where Glomus got the name from. And then Johnny noticed something new: an inscription over the doorway of Glomus's chapel in honor of Sir Robert Shirley, just as there was over the doorway of the original chapel. At the bottom of the page there was an enlarged version of this inscription so it could be easily read. Johnny had studied it before, but he had only half-understood it. Now he read it again.

Suddenly it was as if a light had gone on in his brain. Another part of the puzzle was, maybe, solved.

"Wow!" Johnny exclaimed. He slammed the book shut and got a loud "Shhh!" from the librarian. Normally he would have been embarrassed, but right now nothing mattered except the lost will. He was closer to it than ever. Well, that settled it. He would go tomorrow evening as he had planned, and he would find it.

That evening went by quickly, with dinner, dishes, and homework. After everybody had gone to bed, Johnny got up and started packing his battered cardboard suitcase. He threw in clothes and the big screwdriver from the tool chest in the basement. Then he went downstairs to the kitchen, climbed up on a chair, took down the Prince Albert can, and counted out the money. Johnny still felt very bad about doing this, but he believed it was the only way he could save Gramma's life. With a heavy heart he went back upstairs to finish his packing.

The next morning when Johnny looked out the window, he saw that it was going to be a bright, sunny day. In the sky was a flock of those little gray clouds that have dark bottoms. They always reminded Johnny of boats and made him think of travel.

Downstairs at breakfast he heard on the radio that the first big snowstorm of the winter was sweeping down out of Canada. It would be snowing hard in the White Mountains area by that night. That might put a crimp in things. . . . But, then, weather reports were often wrong —the professor was always saying that. Johnny went hastily over his plans in his mind: He would have to sneak out of the house with his suitcase about half an hour before the train came. Then he would have to hike across town to the railroad station. Should he leave a note of some kind? He'd better, or Gramma and Grampa would think that he had thrown himself into the Merrimack River.

"So, what's on your mind besides hair? Huh?" This was Gramma, who was sitting across from Johnny, munching toast and drinking coffee.

Johnny looked up, alarmed. "Oh, nothin', Gramma," he said quickly. "I was just . . . worryin' about my Latin test."

Gramma snorted. "You can thank your stars that's all you got to worry about," she grumbled. "I hafta go back to the hospital again for more o' them crazy tests. This time it's that hospital over in Amesbury. What's its name, now, Henry?"

"Bon Sekoors," he said, after thinking a second. "French name—dunno what it means, though. We won't be back till after dinnertime, Johnny. Gramma made some sandwiches and put 'em in the icebox for ya."

Johnny looked at Gramma and Grampa. He felt like crying. They were so nice to him, so kind, and here he was running out on them! And with the money out of the can, on top of everything else! They would feel awful when they found out he was gone. How could he tell them that he was doing it all for Gramma?

Johnny went off to school, and the day passed like some sort of strange dream. He felt that everybody was looking at him, that Sister Mary Anthony and all the kids knew what he was up to. Finally, when he walked down the stone steps and out into the sunlight at a quarter past three, Johnny found that he was getting cold feet. He really didn't want to go. It would be so easy just to head home, unpack his suitcase, and relax. Johnny sighed wearily. Yes, that was what he would do, call the whole stupid thing off.

As he walked home Johnny felt better. A great weight had been lifted from his shoulders. He ran quickly up the steps of his house and across the porch and opened the front door. On the kitchen floor lay the day's mail. It must have arrived after Gramma and Grampa had left. As Johnny bent over to pick up the letters, he stiffened. He could see the return address on the businesslike envelope that was lying at the top of the heap:

DIGBY AND COUGHLAN / UNDERTAKERS

Johnny's heart began to pound. He knew what this meant. Gramma was getting ready for her own funeral. She was a very practical, no-nonsense sort of person. And it was just like her to plan the whole business beforehand. A choking sob rose up in Johnny's throat. He couldn't stand by and let something like this happen! The best brain surgeon in the world would be at her side soon if John Michael Dixon had anything to say about it!

Up the stairs he galloped. He tore open the door of his room and then, panting, forced himself to calm down. It was only twenty minutes to four. He had lots of time. First he opened the top drawer of his bureau. Inside lay the wad of bills from the Prince Albert can with a rubber band around it. Next to it was a brass waterproof matchbox with an enameled inset of an Indian's head against the background of a large white star on the lid. This was the lucky matchbox Professor Childermass had given to Johnny. The professor had carried it all through World War One and had come out with only one small injury. *If I ever needed luck, I need it now*, thought Johnny, and he stuck the matchbox in his pocket. He put thirty dollars in his wallet and stuffed the rest into his suitcase, which he dragged out, all packed, from under his bed. He checked its contents once more, then ran downstairs to the basement and came back with an old rusty iron crowbar. After that was packed too, he ran back downstairs to eat the sandwiches they had left for him. Mmmm—roast beef with mustard and mayonnaise! Normally this would have been a real treat, but Johnny's nose was stuffed up, and everything tasted funny. Oh, well—it was food, and he was hungry. He wolfed them down, drank a glass of milk, and then headed upstairs again. He sat down at his desk and wrote the following note:

> Dear Gramma and Grampa,
> I have to do something very important. It is a life or death matter, and it can't wait. I'll be back in a few days, so don't worry. Don't be angry, please. I'll explain everything later.
>
> > Sincerely yours,
> > John
>
> PS: I'm sorry I can't tell you where I'm going. It must remain a secret.

Sadly Johnny took the note downstairs and left it under the sugar bowl. For the last time he tramped back upstairs to his room. With his suitcase in hand and a lump in his throat he wondered when he would see it again. Then quickly he turned, marched out the door and down the stairs. His suitcase banged against the banister as he went. Though Johnny's face was pale and drawn, he looked incredibly determined. He also looked scared.

Professor Childermass had not seen Johnny for a while. And for a good reason—he had been out in Springfield, in the western part of the state, attending his brother's funeral. Having arrived back in Duston Heights on the evening of the fourteenth, dead tired and in a foul mood, he had not wanted to see anyone. But now, twenty-four hours after his return, he was anxious to play a few tough, hard-fought games of chess with Johnny. After fixing an early dinner, he drove up to a candy shop in New Hampshire, bought a pound of dark chocolate creams (they were for Gramma, who loved them), and roared back down Route 125 toward Duston Heights. He pulled up in front of the Dixons' house at just about the time that Johnny was buying his ticket at the railroad station.

The professor jumped out of the car, whistling a jaunty tune. With the candy box in his hand he trotted up the front walk, mounted the steps, threw open the screen door, and marched quickly across the porch. There was a bell, but he preferred to bang on the door with his fist. No answer. He hammered some more and finally in desperation pushed the bell button. Still no answer. "Bah! Phooey!" he said, and started back across the porch. But just then he heard the sound of a motor, saw the flash of headlights, and turned toward the Dixons' car coming into the driveway.

"Ah!" said the professor, grinning, as he ran down the steps to meet his friends. Grampa rolled down his window and peered out.

"That you, Rod?" he called.

"It is, indeed!" intoned the professor. "Who did you think it'd be, the Grand Master of the Knights of St.

John? And I was just about to give up on you folks and go home. By the way, where's John?"

Grampa looked puzzled. "Huh? You mean he's not in the house?"

The professor scowled. "Well, he may be in the bathroom or hiding in the coal cellar. But I am not in the habit of barging into my friends' houses when no one answers the door. Now, then! As soon as you folks can pry yourselves out of your car, let's go in and see if he's anywhere on the premises."

A few minutes later Gramma, Grampa, and the professor were huddled around the dining room table. Gramma was shaking her head, and she was starting to cry. Grampa looked stunned. The flesh of his face sagged, and he seemed very old. The professor, who was standing across the table from Grampa, was holding the note in his trembling hand. The muscle in the corner of his mouth had begun to twitch. Suddenly he threw the note out onto the middle of the table.

"We . . . have . . . got . . . to . . . stay . . . *calm*! LET'S STAY CALM, FOR GOD'S SAKE!" he roared. And to show how calm he was, the professor pounded both fists on the table. The sugar bowl jumped and came down on its side, spilling sugar everywhere. "*Where* on *earth* can he have gone? This is not like him—not like him at all. Oh, John, John, I thought you were so levelheaded and reasonable! Judgment, thou art fled to brutish beasts, and men have lost their reason! Oh, God, God, God!"

Ranting and raving in this way, the professor paced up and down the dining room. Grampa kept staring vacantly into space while Gramma cried silently. Finally the professor stopped and planted himself next to Grampa.

"Henry, you must have *some* idea where he has gone!" he cried out in exasperation.

Grampa turned slowly to face the professor, his cheeks wet with tears. As soon as he saw Grampa's face the professor's attitude changed. He winced, sank down into a chair, and put his head in his hands.

"I'm a cranky old man," he said quietly, through his fingers. "Please forgive me. Now, we must keep our heads and try to figure out where he is." He drew a shuddering breath and wiped his hands over his face. "All right, he can't have gone to Korea to look for his dad, so we can eliminate *that* possibility. I assume he hasn't got enough money to go far. Henry, how much allowance do you give him?"

"A dollar a week," said Grampa wearily. "I wish we could give him more'n that, but . . ." His voice trailed away. A thought had just struck him. "Oh, dear!" he exclaimed, clapping his hand to his forehead. "You don't think . . ."

While the professor stood watching, Grampa went out to the kitchen. There was a sound of scuffling and bumping, and then he came back with the Prince Albert can. He dumped it, upside down, on the table; it was empty.

"A hundred dollars!" he gasped. "He took the hull darned thing! I don't believe it!"

Gramma blew her nose loudly and looked up. "I bet I know what happened," she said in a voice thick with crying. "Some burglar probably broke in an' made Johnny give him the money. Then he held a gun to Johnny's head an' made him write that note. An' then he kidnaped Johnny."

The professor gazed skeptically at Gramma. "Madam," he said solemnly, "not to insult you, but your house is not the sort that would be selected by a burglar, unless that burglar was a nitwit." The professor scratched his nose and gazed abstractedly out the window. Then he snatched up the note and read it again.

"Life-or-death matter . . ." he muttered. "What in blue blazes does *that* mean?" He turned to Grampa. "Henry, would you mind terribly if I went up to Johnny's room and poked around a bit? I might find something that would indicate what he was up to. I mean . . ."

Suddenly the professor's mouth grew wide with alarm. "Great Caesar! You don't suppose . . . but no. He wouldn't! But even so. . . . Look, you two must excuse me for a minute."

And with that the professor ran out into the front hall and dashed up the stairs. Gramma and Grampa watched him through the wide arch that separated the front hall from the dining room. And then they turned and looked at each other in utter astonishment.

CHAPTER ELEVEN

The train whistle blew. It was a long, lonely, mournful sound. Johnny heard it and smiled faintly. He was sitting in a seat near a window, and he felt groggy. Because of his cold and fever, he kept drifting in and out of sleep. He wondered what Gramma and Grampa and the professor were doing. Were they ranting and raving and tearing their hair? Had they called the police? Or were they crying? Johnny felt guilty. *But it's the only way*, he said silently. *It'll all work out—I promise. You'll see, you'll see....*

Johnny looked around. There was only one other passenger in the car, an old lady in a brown winter coat and a flowered babushka. Apparently not many people wanted to travel up to the White Mountains at this time of year. Now a frightening thought struck him: What if the Squam House was closed for the winter? Well, then, he would find some other place to stay.

The door at the end of the car slammed open. A fat man in a blue uniform stepped in.

"Kancamagus Center!" he called out. "This way out!"

It was a little after nine o'clock at night. Johnny dragged himself to his feet, pulled his suitcase down from the overhead rack, and moved toward the door. Steam hissed and billowed around him as he walked down the iron steps. Blearily he looked around. A light was on in the little old-fashioned station, and next to it was a car with an illuminated sign on top that said TAXI. Johnny started to walk faster. Now, if only the cab would take him where he wanted to go!

A few minutes later Johnny's cab pulled up in front of the Squam House. The old inn looked pretty much the way it had when he had seen it last, and the downstairs windows were lit up, which was a hopeful sign. Johnny got out, dragging his suitcase out after him. As he was paying the driver, another wave of fear and loneliness swept over him.

"Is . . . is this place open in the winter?" he asked falteringly.

The driver laughed. "Well, if it ain't, kid, you're gonna hafta sleep under them bushes over there!" Then, when he saw Johnny's scared look, he added, "Old Mrs. Woodley keeps this place open all winter for the rich types who come up here to ski." He looked at Johnny. "By the way, you're kinda young to be ridin' the rails alone, aintcha? What're you up here for?"

Johnny thought quickly. "I'm here to meet my grampa," he said, glancing toward the hotel. "He's coming over from Center Sandwich to get me."

The driver peered at Johnny closely. He seemed to be on the verge of saying something. But he changed his mind, and without another word he rolled up his window and drove off.

Again Johnny felt afraid. But with an effort he pulled himself together, grabbed his suitcase, and walked toward the hotel.

At first there was no answer when he rang the bell. Then Johnny saw a shape moving behind the pleated curtain in the window on his right. The door rattled open, and there stood Mrs. Woodley, looking just as grim and forbidding as Johnny had remembered her being back in October. When she saw who was on her porch, she seemed startled. But then her whole attitude changed. The scowl vanished, and Mrs. Woodley smiled a warm, welcoming smile.

"Why, my goodness!" she exclaimed. "It's the young man from the camp who came to use my phone! What on earth are *you* doing up here? Come in, come in! You'll catch your death of cold out there!"

Johnny was startled by the woman's sudden change in attitude. But he was glad that Mrs. Woodley wasn't throwing him out. Incredibly tired, feverish, and sniffly, he lugged his suitcase in and set it down by the reception desk. Mrs. Woodley told him to wait there, that she'd be back in a minute. She disappeared into a back room, and Johnny stood by the desk. He dug his hand into his parka pocket, and it closed over something cold and hard—the lucky matchbox. Johnny pulled the matchbox out and fiddled with it. Rubbing the smooth surface comforted him somehow.

When Mrs. Woodley returned, she was holding a guest book bound in green leather and a fountain pen. She set the book down in front of Johnny and handed him the pen. Johnny paused before signing. Should he use a fake name? No, it was possible that Mrs. Woodley remembered his real name. Bending over the book, he signed *Johnny Dixon* slowly and carefully.

Mrs. Woodley went on chattering while he signed the book. "Well, it certainly is nice to have guests this time of year!" she said cheerfully. "This is the in-between season, you know. The leaves are off the trees, and the snow hasn't fallen yet. What are you up here for, by the way? If you don't mind my asking, that is?"

Johnny laid down the pen and glanced distrustfully at Mrs. Woodley. He did not like this incredible cheeriness. *Was she putting on an act or what?* As for the question about what he was doing, Johnny had figured it was coming, sooner or later. And he had an answer ready—the same one that he had given the taxi driver.

"I uh, I'm gonna meet my grampa. He lives near here, over in Center Sandwich. He's gonna come over and get me tomorrow, soon's he can. He, uh, he might be late on account of his . . . his cow is sick." Rather unnecessarily Johnny added, "He, uh, he lives on a farm."

Johnny paused and waited for Mrs. Woodley's reaction. He had pored over a road map on the way up, and he had picked Center Sandwich because it didn't look like it was on any railway line. Would Mrs. Woodley fall for this little fib?

Apparently she would. Closing the guest book, she gazed placidly at Johnny. "Well, young man, you're welcome to stay here as long as you need to. You're my only guest at present, and I'll show you all the hospitality that I can. Have you had dinner?"

Johnny had eaten before he left home. But that didn't matter—he still felt hungry. "Uh, no, I . . . I haven't," he muttered, looking around stupidly. "Can I get something to eat?"

Once again Mrs. Woodley was all grandmotherly kindness. "Why, of course you can! Good heavens, and you've got a cold too! You're supposed to eat well when you have a cold—it builds up your resistance. Come on, now, let's go out to the kitchen and see what we can find."

And, clucking and crooning like the Queen of All Grandmothers, Mrs. Woodley led Johnny out of the lobby and down a short hall that smelled of wood smoke and into a big, old-fashioned kitchen.

Later, after Johnny had finished his meal, Mrs. Woodley took him upstairs to his room. It was a comfortable room with white woodwork and a high walnut bed. Over the bureau hung a little picture that seemed odd to Johnny. It showed an eye shining out of a pyramid, and on top of the pyramid was a motto:

Thou God seest ME

After Mrs. Woodley had explained to Johnny where the bathroom was and told him to sleep well, she left, closing the door softly behind her. Johnny was alone. He looked around the room. Except for the weird picture, it seemed very homey and friendly. He ought to be worn out and ready for bed, but for some reason he wasn't. Something inside him was humming like a dynamo, keeping him keyed up and wide awake. He threw his suitcase on the bed and started taking things out of it and putting them in the drawers of the bureau. When the suitcase was empty—except for the crowbar, the screwdriver, and the flashlight—Johnny snapped it shut and stood it in a corner. He folded down the bed covers and fluffed up the pillow. Still there was this humming in his ears. Still there was a voice inside him saying, *Watch out. There's something wrong.*

Johnny felt frustrated and puzzled. Unless he got some sleep tonight, he would be a total wreck tomorrow when he was supposed to go out to the estate and hunt for the will. He went to the bureau and got out his pajamas. He laid them on the bed, and he was just starting to unbutton his shirt when he had a silly, ungovernable urge to play with his flashlight. Johnny laughed.

Ever since he was a small kid, he had loved flashlights. He'd owned a wonderful old-fashioned one once, with a long, nickel-plated handle that he would shine out his bedroom window at night for fun. This flashlight had had a blinker button on it, and Johnny had used it to send pretend Morse code messages from imaginary spies or people on sinking ships. Maybe playing with the flashlight now would help him relax. Johnny went to the suitcase and snapped it open. With the flashlight in his hand he moved to the window.

It was a small, slightly crooked sash window, but with some shoving Johnny got it to slide up. Cold air flowed in, and Johnny shivered. He snapped on the flashlight and shone it out into a mass of pine trees in the distance. The circle of light moved over banks of dark green needles. *Flash-flash-flash.* Johnny pushed the button— this flashlight had one too—and imaginary messages leaped out into the night. *Ship sinking. Send Help.* What Johnny was really sending with his flasher was just *dah-dit, dah-dit, dit-dit-dit-dah.* This was Morse for CV, the initials of Champagne Velvet, the champagne of bottled beer. He had gotten it from the radio commercials, and he sent it over and over again. But this little routine soon got boring. Now Johnny wanted to see how far the flashlight's beam would carry. He could just barely make out, in the open space beyond the pines, the side of a white clapboard house. Would the beam reach it? He held his arm out the window, stretching as far as he could. Despite his efforts, the shaft of light died before it could reach the house. Sighing, Johnny snapped the flashlight off and jerked his arm back. But as he did this, the tip of his elbow struck the sill. His arm went numb, his hand opened, and the flashlight fell.

"Darn!" Johnny yelled. Annoyed, he peered down at the ground, where there were several little bushes. Maybe they had broken the fall. If the flashlight was smashed . . . well, Johnny didn't want to think about that. Hastily he ducked his head back inside the window and slid the sash down. He went to the closet, got out his coat, and put it on. Then, moving slowly and cautiously, he opened the door and stepped out into the hall. It was true that he was the only guest in the hotel, but he certainly didn't want Mrs. Woodley to hear him. He tiptoed down the hall and down the narrow back staircase. The steps complained loudly, but there was not much that Johnny could do about that. At the bottom of the stairs there was a door with a bolt on the inside. Johnny drew back the bolt, opened the door, and moved out into the chilly, dark yard. Suddenly he had a thought. He went back, found a brick, and stuck it in the door.

Twigs and gravel crunched under his feet as he picked his way around the corner of the building. Now he was on the side of the inn where his window was. Stooped over, he sidled along, rubbing his rear against the foundation stones. It was pitch black. With his hand Johnny combed the top of a low juniper bush. Nothing there. Well, on to the next one. . . . Ah! There it was, lying on a soft, springy bush, as neat as could be! Johnny reached out and picked the flashlight up. He clicked it on and off. It worked. He heaved a deep sigh of relief and was about to start back toward the door he had come out of when suddenly he froze.

A voice was speaking, somewhere above him. It was Mrs. Woodley's voice, drifting out through a partly opened window. Johnny held his breath and listened. At first it just sounded like a wordless muttering, but as he listened more intently Johnny could make out what the old woman was saying. And the words made the hairs on the back of his neck stand on end.

CHAPTER TWELVE

❧❀❧

"Chad? Chad? Is that you?" said the cracked, querulous voice. "You've come to stare at me again, have you? Well, my fine young nephew—my *former* nephew, I suppose I should say—I've put up with worse things in my time than your homely face peering down at me. When I learned to control the Guardian, I did some things that you would have run screaming away from when you were alive. Go ahead, shake your head, see if I care! I know, I'm supposed to feel guilty because I put you out of the way. Well, I don't. I have some rights in this life. I've worked hard, and I deserve to have some comforts in my old age. If I had let you find my dear brother's will—and you were just the one who might have done it—what would have happened to me? Answer me that! What if the will had said that dear Herbert had cut me off without a cent? At least, without the will I get *something*! And that, dear boy, is why you had to leave us. I don't know if you were close to finding it. But I wasn't going to take any chances—no sirree!"

Mrs. Woodley had stopped talking. Johnny heard the faint sound of perhaps a bed or chair creaking, a coughing noise, and then the old woman's voice again. "Don't look at me like that, please. I know you feel bad, but there's nothing I can do about it, is there? You were a reckless and irresponsible young man, and well, what's done is done. And I'll tell you something else. There's somebody who's going to be joining you soon. It's that little snot, that boy who was up here last month. You remember—the one I sent that little greeting card to, to try and warn him off? Yes, he's here right now, staying at my hotel!"

Mrs. Woodley laughed, a nasty, sneering laugh. "Yes, and he's after the will. How do I know? Well, when he was here in October, he made a phone call at my hotel, and it so happens that I can read lips. Of course he had no idea that I understood every word he was saying. Yes, he's figured out a great deal, and I'm sure he'd find the will, if I were to let him continue. But just between you and me let me tell you something: He's not going to get anywhere near it, because tomorrow morning he's going to meet with a little accident, and then he'll be where you are. Just think! You'll have some company! Won't that be nice?"

Silence. Johnny crouched under the windowsill. Sweat was pouring down his face, and his body felt goose-pimply all over. So Mrs. Woodley was Mr. Glomus's sister! She knew the will was up there on the estate, and she had killed Chad—or had she? Maybe she was just crazy. She was just talking to herself, or . . .

At that moment Johnny saw something—saw it and felt it too. It was like a gray luminous fog, a hovering cloud shaped like a human being. It drifted out of Mrs. Woodley's bedroom window, and as it moved away Johnny felt icy cold. His scalp tingled, his heart beat faster, and he found it hard to breathe. The shape moved off into the darkness, hovered by the pines, and then faded into nothing.

Johnny closed his eyes and shuddered convulsively. He wished with all his heart that he had never come up here. He wanted to be home safe in his bed. But he wasn't at home. He was up here in New Hampshire, out in the cold and dark, staying in a hotel run by a woman who was planning to kill him. What should he do? He wanted to run off suddenly into the night and hide down by the railroad station till a train came. But his money was up in the dresser drawer in his room. Everything was up there, including the tools he was going to use during his search for the will. Was he going to have to give up on his search, then, to escape from this wicked old woman who seemed to have some kind of supernatural powers?

But Johnny was a pretty strong person, in spite of his timidity. He was panicked, scared half out of his mind, but as he huddled there against the wall he fought it down. Once again his old determination came back.

Johnny thought hard. Many times in chess games he had tried to figure out what his opponent would do next so that he could outwit him. Now he tried to figure out what Mrs. Woodley was going to do. Nothing, probably, for the time being. Tomorrow morning, when he was getting ready to go out to the Glomus estate to poke around—that was when she said she would try to stop him. All right, then, he would mess up her plans. He would escape tonight. He'd just have to go back upstairs and get a few things—the crowbar, the screwdriver, his money, and the map of the roads around Lake Chocorua. Could he summon up enough courage to go back up there? Johnny bit his lip. He closed his eyes, took a deep breath and let it out slowly. Yes, he was ready now. He had to go back.

Cautiously Johnny moved down the wall, scuttling sideways like a crab and gripping the precious flashlight tight in his hand. Around the corner he went and then straightened up to open the door. He set the doorstop aside. Soundlessly he let the door close, and then up the stairs he tiptoed. More creaking—he couldn't stop that. Then down the hall to his room. Johnny slipped inside, closed the door, and let out a deep sigh of relief. Quickly, darting this way and that, he moved about the little room, gathering up the things he needed. Crowbar. Screwdriver. Map. Money. Wallet. Finally he was ready to go again.

It wasn't far to Mount Chocorua and the Glomus estate. Johnny had a fairly good sense of direction, and once he got out onto Route 16, he thought he would remember which way to go. Fearfully he eyed the door of his room. What might be waiting for him outside? With an effort he jerked it open. Nothing but the musty carpeted hallway. Johnny made the sign of the cross, awkwardly, because he was still holding the flashlight, then out into the hall he went.

For hours the professor's car had been speeding along on New Hampshire State Route 16. The professor was behind the wheel, hunched over, gripping it tightly. In his mouth was an unlit Sobranie cigarette, and on his face was a look of crabby determination. A scrubby old deerstalker's cap was on his head, and the fur-lined flaps were tied down over his ears. Sitting next to the professor was Fergie Ferguson. The professor had persuaded him to come along because he was convinced that Fergie could help him find Johnny. After dashing madly from the Dixons' house with some "clues" crammed into his pocket, the professor had driven with lightning speed across town to the Fergusons'. He had barged in on them in the middle of their dinner and, after frightening poor Mrs. Ferguson half to death, had managed to convince the family that he badly needed Fergie's help. The professor was a good guesser. He had found some stationery from the Squam House in Johnny's bureau and was sure that Johnny was after the Glomus will. Then, guessing wildly this time, the professor had decided that maybe Johnny and Fergie knew something about it that they weren't telling him. So after taking Fergie into a back room of the Ferguson home, he gave him the good old-fashioned third degree. At first Fergie had refused to tell him anything. But then, when he realized that Johnny's life might be in danger, he changed his mind and told him about the strange midnight meeting with Chad Glomus and Chad's terrifying disappearance. That was all the professor needed. He persuaded the puzzled Fergusons that their son ought to go with him. They were reluctant to give their permission at first, but the professor pleaded and wheedled. He also added that there was no danger involved—this was not true, but the professor was not above lying to get something he wanted. Finally the Fergusons had insisted that the police be contacted. And the professor had said blandly that of course he intended to do so immediately. This was another lie—for reasons of his own the professor had no intention of bringing the police into this strange and desperate manhunt.

On roared the professor's car. He was a terror on wheels, even when he wasn't on a life-or-death mission. He jammed the accelerator down, and the needle flicked past ninety. Fergie sat rigidly, gripping the edge of the seat with his hands. Once he had ridden with Father Higgins, the parish priest at St. Michael's. He had been bad, but he hadn't been anything like this.

"Professor?" said Fergie in a tight, strained voice. "How . . . how far do we have to go?"

"Oh, not so far now. That town we just passed through is Center Ossipee. It's only about twelve miles to Kancamagus Center. We'll get there soon—don't worry."

Now the tires squeeched loudly as the car rounded a difficult S-curve. Fergie was thrown first against the door, then back the other way.

"Where do you think he'd go?" the professor barked out suddenly without taking his eyes off the road.

Fergie thought hard. "Gee. I dunno. Did you say he bought a ticket at the train station?"

"Yes. I checked there because it was the only possible way for Johnny to get up to that idiotic estate. The ticket was to Kancamagus Center. Could he walk out to the Glomus place from there?"

Fergie thought some more. "Maybe, only I don't think he would want to, unless he's *really* flipped his lid. I bet he'll just sack out somewhere for the night, and then bomb on out to the old estate in the morning."

The professor considered Fergie's suggestion. He grimaced, as he often did when he was thinking, and the cigarette bobbed up and down in his mouth. "Hmm. I think, Byron, that you are most probably right. After all, John doesn't know that anyone is following him, and he can certainly afford to pay for a room. Did I tell you that he swiped about a hundred dollars from his grandparents before he lit out?"

"Yeah, you did. That's not so great."

The professor opened his mouth to sigh, but as he did the cigarette fell out. "Blast!" he snapped. Then he shook his head, and his face tensed up. "I certainly hope he's all right," he said softly, and he pushed the accelerator pedal down harder.

CHAPTER THIRTEEN

❦

A short time later the professor's car came rolling into Kancamagus Center, where houses, trees, steeples, the wide grassy common, all were still and dreamlike on this frosty November night. The sky was clear, and you would never have guessed that a snowstorm was on its way. But snow was what the weatherman on the radio had said. The professor had heard the report more than once today, and it had filled his mind with fear for Johnny's safety. Now he pulled over to the curb next to the deserted common, turned the motor off, and heaved a small sigh. After some fumbling in the glove compartment, he found his pack of Balkan Sobranie cigarettes and lit one.

"So, Byron," he said, turning to Fergie. "I wonder what our next move ought to be. If we are right, Johnny is holed up somewhere here in town. This Squam House —the one whose letter paper Johnny had—is probably our best bet, don't you agree?"

Fergie nodded. "Yeah, I guess so. We could ask the lady that runs the place if he's there. Only it's really late, an' Johnny told me that she's an unbelievable witch. I think she'd raise hell if we was just to go up an' hammer on her door now."

The professor turned on the dome light in his car. He peered at his watch, which said ten after twelve, and then flipped the light off. "Ye-es," he said slowly, considering, "I imagine she would get into a bit of a snit if we woke her up now. Unfortunately, however, I am a very impatient sort, and I am not going to sit here smoking cigarettes and fidgeting until the dawn's early light. So Mrs. Whosis will just have to get herself into a Grade-A snit. We are going over there *now!*"

And with that the professor turned the ignition key. The car sprang to life. But then, abruptly, the professor turned the motor off.

"What's wrong?" Fergie asked anxiously.

"Nothing much. I just realized I don't know where that idiotic inn is." Suddenly an idea struck him. He turned the dome light on, again reached over and dug into the glove compartment, and came out with a wrinkled piece of letter paper. He uncrumpled it, and Fergie saw that it was a piece of the Squam House's stationery. At the top was a picture of the inn in green ink, and down below was the motto *The friendly white inn on the common.*

The professor's mouth curled into a sarcastic grin. "Friendly, eh? Well, we shall see."

The professor started up his car again. Slowly the battered old Ford crawled along the dark street, which was getting darker by the minute as black clouds rushed in to cover the moon. The professor peered out the car window owlishly as he examined one blank staring house front, then crept on to the next one and the next one. Finally, with a look of triumph on his face, he put on the brakes. There was the inn, identical to its picture on the letterhead. Although a carriage lamp on a post was shining out in front, the windows were dark.

The professor turned off the motor and sat with arms folded. Looking out at the inn, he shook his head slowly. "She's going to be in a rare mood when we wake her up," he said. "But I'm afraid there's no help for it. Come on, Byron—unless, of course, you'd rather stay in the car."

"Naw, I'll come," said Fergie, grinning maliciously. He thought it might be fun to see a nasty old woman after she had been awakened out of a sound sleep.

Two car doors slammed. Walking side by side, Fergie and the professor strode up the walk, up the steps, and onto the wide porch. The professor harrumphed in a nervous way and jabbed at the bell with his index finger. It was a loud bell, and they could hear it ringing deep inside the inn. At first nothing happened. Fergie rubbed his mittened hands and the professor puffed his cigarette and sang "*Cadet Roussel*," a French nonsense song that he liked. But soon lights began to come on. There was the sound of chains rattling, and then the door swung open. Mrs. Woodley stood before them, wearing a blue quilted dressing gown with a little ruffled collar and holding a small black flashlight. Cold cream covered her face, and she looked very, very angry.

"Well?" she said. Her voice trembled with indignation as she eyed the two of them. "You've gotten me up in the middle of the night—I congratulate you. What do you want?"

Normally the professor was able to hold his own against even the crankiest and most forbidding people. But there was a strange aura about Mrs. Woodley that suggested . . . well, something more than ordinary nastiness. The professor took a step backward, and there was genuine fear in his eyes. But then he pulled himself together and put on his most brusque and businesslike manner.

"Madam," he said crisply, "I deeply apologize for waking you out of a sound sleep on such a cold night and at such a late hour. But the fact is, this is somewhat of an emergency. We are looking for a young man named John Dixon. He's about twelve, and he's pale, blond, and wears glasses. We have reason to believe that he came up here by train and intended to spend the night at your, uh, establishment. Is he here?"

Mrs. Woodley's mind was racing. If she told this man

that the boy was here, then he'd take the boy away, and she'd be rid of him, wouldn't she? But he might come back. No, it would be better to be rid of him once and for all.

"There's nobody staying here tonight but me," she said in her grimmest, most final tone. "I don't get much business at this time of year. Now, if that is all you have to say to me . . ."

Mrs. Woodley stepped back and took hold of the edge of the door, getting ready to shut the two intruders out. But the professor had been watching her like a hawk, and he thought he saw something in her eyes that suggested she might be lying. With a sudden spring he leapt forward and planted both feet on the doorsill.

Mrs. Woodley's mouth dropped open. "I beg your *pardon!*" she began, her voice rising an octave or two.

"Thank you, I accept your invitation," snapped the professor, and with that he shoved rudely past Mrs. Woodley and dashed into the lighted lobby of the inn. This was a desperate gamble on the professor's part. He wanted to get inside to see if he could find something, anything that would prove that Johnny had been there. Wildly the professor looked this way and that. He took in the couches, the easy chairs, the fussy mahogany tables with oil lamps and bric-a-brac on them. But meanwhile Mrs. Woodley was advancing on him, bubbling over with rage.

"*Now, see here, you!*" she yelled. "*What do you think gives you the right to come barging in here and—*"

"Ah-*hah!*" screeched the professor. He leaped toward the reception desk and swept up something in his right hand. He held it up triumphantly between his thumb and index finger. It was Johnny's waterproof matchbox. "So he *was* here after all! And you were lying to me, you foul-tempered old bat! *Lying!*"

The professor waved his accusing finger in Mrs. Woodley's face. But now she had grown dangerously calm. She folded her arms and glowered at him. "That matchbox is mine," she said grimly. "And you are trespassing. I'll thank you to give it back to me, take that ugly little snot over there, and leave *right now*, before I call the police!"

As Fergie watched the professor and Mrs. Woodley facing each other down in the middle of the room, the air between them seemed to shimmer with tension. The professor held the matchbox up and waved it back and forth before Mrs. Woodley's eyes.

"You deny that this is Johnny's?" he shouted, in a voice that was rising in pitch with every instant. "You actually *deny it?*"

Mrs. Woodley glared stonily, saying nothing. A sudden evil inspiration darted into the professor's head. He turned on his heel and strode to the long polished table that stood between the two rows of armchairs. On it was a group of carefully arranged objects: Staffordshire china dogs and cats, glass paperweights, a blue glass medicine bottle, and a Dresden figurine of a minstrel playing a mandolin. The professor remembered now the story Johnny had told him about the fussy old lady who was afraid he would break the vase on her phone table. With a sudden swoop he reached out and picked up a small china dog, wheeled around, and threw it into the fireplace. The dog shattered into thousands of tiny white pieces.

"There!" said the professor with a snort of satisfaction. He turned back to Mrs. Woodley. "Now, then! If you don't want something like that to happen again, you malignant old hag, I suggest that you tell me what you have done with Johnny!"

Mrs. Woodley's face was a mask of cold hatred, and a vein in her neck was throbbing. Suddenly she flicked out her left hand, and as she did this the professor felt a sharp stab of numbing pain. His right hand—which he had used to throw the dog—felt as if an enormous bee had stung it. Clutching the throbbing hand to his chest, the professor reeled back. His eyes were wide with fear.

"That's what you get," crooned the old woman maliciously, "for willfully destroying private property!" Now her tone became harder, angrier. She advanced on the professor, and he retreated, still clutching his wounded hand. "Get out of here!" she snarled. "Get out of here, and don't come back!"

The professor and Fergie did not need any more encouragement. Fergie went first, and the professor dashed after him, slamming the door as he went. Together they stumbled down the stairs, and they were halfway down the walk before Mrs. Woodley emerged on the porch. Her face was purple with rage, and little white flecks of foam appeared at the corners of her mouth.

"If you ever find him, you may not like what you see!" she screeched in a voice that was scarcely human. *"And if you try to meddle in things that don't concern you, you'll wish you hadn't!"* With that she stepped back and slammed the door loudly. The thunderous sound seemed to reverberate in the still, frosty night air. Then there was silence, and the lights inside the inn went out.

The professor and Fergie stood by the car, staring in wide-eyed horror at the darkened building. Neither of them said anything for a long while.

Finally the professor spoke. "My God! I never imagined . . . I mean, who could possibly have guessed . . . ?"

Fergie glanced nervously back at the inn. He tugged at the professor's arm. "Come on. Let's get outa here before she comes back and really takes care of us."

The professor nodded. They ran around the car and jumped in.

"I'm going to have to do this one-handed for a bit," said the professor, gasping with pain. "It'll be awkward, but I'll manage." He turned the key and the motor started. Then, bracing his left arm against the wheel and shifting gears with his right, he got the car going. It moved in a wobbly, uncertain way, and he nosed it around to the other side of the common. Then he pulled over to the curb, turned off the motor, and just sat staring blankly at the windshield.

Fergie was worried. Maybe the professor was sick, or dying. "Are . . . are you okay, sir?" he asked falteringly.

"No," intoned the professor. Then he laughed and smiled reassuringly. "In my mind I am blowing up the Squam House with sticks of dynamite. But except for that, I am as well as can be expected, as my sickly aunt Sally always used to say. But what do we do now? *That* is what I want to know!"

Fergie also tried hard to think. "Is she a witch?" he asked at last.

The professor groaned. "Oh, God! Let's not go into that! She's a . . . a *something*, that's for bloody sure!" And with his good hand he pounded on the steering wheel.

"Do you suppose she's holdin' Johnny prisoner?" Fergie asked. "I mean, bound and gagged in a cellar or . . . or somethin' like that?"

The professor shook his head. "No. No, I don't think so. That last thing she shrieked, about 'if you ever find him' . . . that says to me that he's out there in the dark somewhere. No, he must have escaped from her—for now, anyway. That may be why she's so incredibly angry. We can't be sure of anything, of course. But first of all I guess we'd better head out to that awful estate . . . Tooting Stanton, or whatever its name is. If Johnny is anywhere, he's out there. And I hope, I very much hope that we can get in by way of that secret passage that you told me about. Do you think you can direct me to the estate?" Fergie nodded. "I . . . I guess so, Professor Childermass. It's dark, but once we get to the road that goes out to the camp, I think it'll look kinda familiar."

The professor flipped on the headlights and started the motor. "I hope so," he said. Then he put the car in gear and roared away in a cloud of exhaust smoke.

Meanwhile, up in her bedroom, Mrs. Woodley was dragging a strange, bulky object from her closet. It was like a small square chest covered with cracked, goose-pimply leather. Muttering unpleasantly to herself, the old woman folded the top back and part of the front down. Now the box resembled a small stage on which miniature actors might move about. It was dark inside but . . . No! Mrs. Woodley said a word, and it started to glow with a quivering blue light. Strange signs and a picture of a comet with a long flaring tail slowly became visible on the wood. In a row on the tiny stage stood several glass bottles. One was tall and thin, one was pear-shaped, one was very small, and another was all bulbs with a long spout projecting from it. A hissing blue flame shot from the spout, making all the bottles glow. Twisted strands and loops of fire burned inside each one—purple, red, orange, yellow. From a drawer in the front of the box Mrs. Woodley took a small metal holy-water sprinkler. She shook drops over the glowing bottles, and they began to shiver and send up a high-pitched wailing music, like the sound of a glass harmonica. Suddenly a formless patch of golden light appeared on the wall behind the box. In the center of the patch of light was a pyramid with an eye in its center. And over the pyramid were some Hebrew letters glowing with red fire. The mingled colored lights flitted about Mrs. Woodley's face as she stared at them intently. Her lips formed strange phrases, and an incantation rose to mingle with the bottles' eerie wail.

Johnny walked quickly along a dark, gravelly road that cut through great masses of trees. It led from Camp Chocorua to the old estate, and it was a road that he remembered well. Passing through the deserted picnic grounds by dark, still Lake Chocorua had been strange. Although he had not been able to see the mountain itself, he had felt its looming presence. Johnny was surprised to find out what a good hiker he was. Maybe the week in October had done him some good. Whatever the reason, he had covered the three miles in a relatively short time.

His head cold was still a problem, of course. Every now and then he had to set down his crowbar and fish his handkerchief out of his pocket so he could blow his nose. But he wasn't collapsing or anything. He felt strong and brave and purposeful, even though the fear of Mrs. Woodley hovered in the back of his mind.

Johnny slowed down. He played the flashlight's pale beam along the left-hand side of the road as he searched for the little stone that marked the path to the lodge.

Had he come too far? No! There it was, half-buried in leaves. He felt a triumphant surge in his chest. He was doing it! He was on his way!

Johnny turned onto the path and walked on, peering into the darkness as he went. It was easier to see through the trees now that they were bare. In the distance he could make out the quaint steep-gabled cottage with its gothic doodads and carvings. Rushing toward it now, Johnny felt something cold hit his cheek. Snow! Oh, well, it wasn't coming down very hard. As Johnny tramped on, swinging the crowbar jauntily, the lodge drew closer and closer until finally he was standing before it.

Johnny laughed. He felt like Hansel and Gretel at the old witch's cottage. The lodge was like that, a weird fairy-tale house that an old witch might live in. What if he opened the door and found Mrs. Woodley standing there, grinning evilly at him? Johnny shuddered. He really did not like thoughts like that.

After a quick nervous look around, Johnny set the crowbar down next to the doorway. He played the flashlight beam along the row of carved stone ballflowers that ran along the lintel over the door. *Which one had it been?* Ah . . . that one, with the hole in it! Standing on tiptoe, Johnny reached in and pulled out the small, old-fashioned key, fit it into the lock, and heaved open the door. Then he picked up the crowbar and stepped inside.

The room was as musty and dismal and empty as it had been before. Mr. Glomus leered down at him from his frame over the mantel, and for the thousandth time Johnny thought about what a very strange old coot he must have been. However, he had not come here to think about Mr. Glomus. He was here on business.

Johnny examined the front of the fireplace. The smiling children with their cereal bowls gazed blandly down at him. One of those heads was the knob. One, two, three . . . the third one up from the right looked slightly worn. Cautiously Johnny reached up and tried to twist the head. It moved. To his great delight Johnny heard the grumbling of machinery, of hidden chains and counterweights. Slowly, inch by inch, the massive stone slab at the back of the hearth rose up. But then, quite suddenly, the noise stopped. The slab was stuck! By the light of the flashlight Johnny could see a dark opening that was only about a foot high.

Johnny sighed. He knelt down and shuffled on his knees into the mouth of the fireplace to inspect the narrow opening. Could he fit through it? Well, he would have to. First he slid the all-important crowbar into the opening as far as it would go. Then, with his flashlight in his hand, he flattened himself on the floor, wriggled forward over the sooty hearthstone, and squeezed himself through.

On the other side Johnny pulled himself to his feet. For a moment he thought about searching for the lever that would make the slab go back down. But it occurred to him that he might want to come back this way, and if he closed the door, he might—for all he knew—be closing it for good. So Johnny brushed the soot off the front of his parka and picked up the crowbar once more. With the flashlight beam playing before him, he advanced into the dank, foul-smelling tunnel.

Johnny moved forward through the dark. Suddenly, for no reason at all, he remembered his matchbox. He felt in his pockets. Oh, no! It was gone! He had probably left it back at the inn. No time to go back now, though. He pressed on. And now the fear of the Guardian began to creep over him. Inside his head he heard Chad Glomus's horrible screams and remembered what he had said: "The Guardian might be anything: It might be a pool of moonlight on the floor, or a chair, or smoke drifting in the air. It will come for you if you get too close to the will. . . ."

Johnny tried to laugh his fear off. He tried to believe what Fergie believed, and he told himself stubbornly that Chad's disappearance had been faked. He was rich and screwy, and right now he was probably drinking a gin and tonic in a bar in Bermuda. Anything was possible if you were rich, Johnny told himself. But then he thought of the things he had seen and heard when he was crouching under Mrs. Woodley's window, and the fear crept back, chilling him to the bone.

Johnny kept walking. He went up two broad shallow steps to the second level of the tunnel, till he finally saw, far ahead, the stout nail-studded door that led to the crypt beneath the chapel. He stopped, listening for sounds. Nothing. The silence was complete and abso-

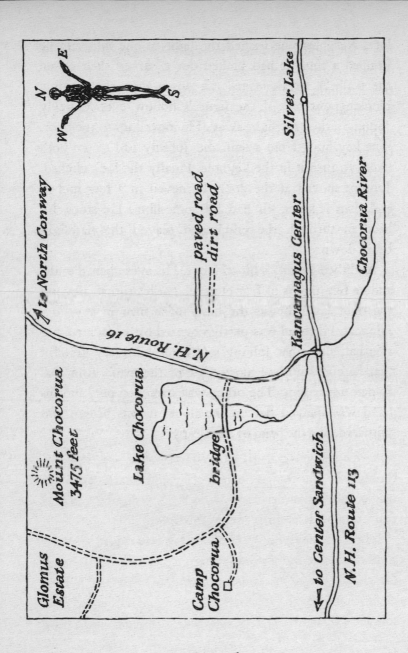

lute. Nervously he flashed the light to one side, and he jumped a foot. It had picked out a carved skeleton on the wall. A streak of ice ran down over the carving, blocking out one of the figure's hollow eyes. Quickly Johnny jerked the light away. He moved up to the door. The key hung from a nail, and Johnny had to use both hands to turn it in the keyhole. Finally the lock clicked. Johnny shoved at the door. It moved in a few inches, and then it stuck—it had hit something. He stuck his head in through the crack and played the flashlight beam down.

And then Johnny's blood froze. His eyes opened wide, and he felt fingers of fear clutching at his throat. Beyond the door lay a body, the body of a man in a yellow raincoat. His head was partly covered by a black rubber rain hat, and what Johnny saw made him very grateful that he could not see more. One of the man's arms was folded under him. The other was stretched out, and his hand was splayed flat on the floor. It was brown and withered, like the hand of a mummy.

CHAPTER FOURTEEN

Johnny closed his eyes. A wave of sick terror swept over him. He was afraid that he would faint, or die. But his resolve was strong, and he summoned up all the courage that was in him.

When he opened his eyes, the horrible shape was still there, sprawled on the cold stones. In the midst of his panic Johnny felt terribly sorry for Chad. He had been peculiar, but he had tried to be nice to Johnny and Fergie. He hadn't been particularly likable, but he hadn't been evil. Johnny swallowed hard, and another sick, convulsive shudder ran through his body. This cleared his head, somehow. He had no time to get upset, not now. He had to press on, and if the Guardian caught up with him . . . well, at least he would go down fighting. Johnny got a good tight grip on the crowbar and the flashlight. Then, turning his eyes away, he edged around the slumped body and flashed his light this way and that. The crypt was a low, gloomy chamber, a sort of basement under the chapel. Rows of stone arches stretched away into the distance. *Was there a door that led upstairs?* There had to be. Johnny crept forward cautiously, past heavy round pillars. Ahead, at the top of a low flight of stone steps, he saw what he was looking for. Up the steps he went. The door opened easily, and he found that he was peering into a narrow stairwell. More steps corkscrewed upward. He followed them, and at the top was yet another door. He opened it and found that he was in the chapel.

Because it was dark, Johnny had only a dim idea of what the place looked like. He played the flashlight beam about and saw high wooden pews, a stone altar with a bronze crucifix on it, and a series of gothic arches that marched down the side aisles. Johnny loved strange old buildings, and at another time he might have stopped to explore. But he was in a hurry. So, putting on a look of the grimmest determination, he tramped purposefully down the aisle. At the back of the chapel, under the organ loft, was a big, pointed wooden door with two leaves that were held together by a bolt in the middle. There were spring bolts at the top and the bottom. Johnny slid them back. He pulled the handle and the door swung outward. Cold air rushed in, and snowflakes stung Johnny's face. He was out in the open air again at last.

Johnny felt grateful and extremely relieved. He just stood there a moment, eyes closed, and let the tiny frigid white dots hit his face. He had not been cooped up in the tunnel and the crypt for very long, but it had seemed like ages. Greedily he gulped cold air into his lungs. Johnny wanted to stand there forever, but he knew he couldn't. Doggedly he dragged his mind back to the job that was at hand.

Johnny picked his way down the short flight of steps that led to the open space in front of the chapel. He turned and glanced to his right. Beyond the swirling snow he could just barely see the vast black shadow of the mansion. Before him rose the chapel's tower, a stubby structure with battlements on top. Although the church was gothic, the doorway was classical. It was flanked by fluted pillars with scrolled capitals, and there was a fancy stone cornice over the door. Above the cornice was a triangular stone slab called a pediment. Set in its center was a square tablet made of white marble, and on the tablet was the inscription that had excited Johnny so much when he'd read it for the second time in the book he had found in the library. He had copied the inscription out of the book and had pored over it on the train ride up to New Hampshire. In the dark Johnny could not make out the inscription. Nevertheless he could have recited it by heart:

In the yeare 1653 when
all thinges Sacred were throughout ye nation
Either demolisht or profaned
Sir Robert Shirley, Barronet,
Founded this church;
Whose singular praise it is,
to haue done the best things in ye worst times,
and
hoped them in the most callamitous.
The righteous shall be had
in everlasting remembrance.

Johnny loved the inscription. It sounded grand and
thrilling, even though he didn't know anything about Sir
Robert Shirley or the calamitous times that he had lived
in. He was also filled with smug self-satisfaction, because he had figured out that the *ye* in YE OLDE TEA
SHOPPE referred to the two *ye*'s in the inscription. He
even knew, thanks to the professor, that *ye* in the old
days was sometimes just a funny way of writing *the*. But
Johnny didn't have time to pat himself on the back. He
had to find some way of getting up to the place where
the inscription was so he could examine it more closely.

With a sinking heart Johnny realized that this was not
a part of the treasure hunt that he had planned very carefully. Were there any ladders around? He hadn't seen
any, and ladders were not the kinds of things that people left lying about on a deserted estate in the winter-
time. Then suddenly Johnny grinned. He had been staring at the solution all the time. A mass of ivy vines grew

up one side of the carved doorway, twisting about the columns till they spread their hundreds of spidery tendrils across the inscribed stone tablet at the top. And there was even a little ledge under the tablet. If he ever got up that high, Johnny was sure he could stand on it.

Johnny took off his gloves and put them into a pocket of his parka. Then he reached out, took hold of the vines, and started to climb. It turned out to be surprisingly easy. The vines were spread out all across the face of the doorway, and Johnny found handholds and footholds everywhere. And so, before long, Johnny was stepping out onto the narrow ledge that stood atop the doorway. He was still clinging to the vines for dear life, terribly afraid he might slip. But when he finally had a firm footing on the ledge, he let go. Now he was standing over the doorway of the church. It was not a terribly long way down, but even so, if he had taken a step backward, he would have had a pretty nasty fall. Johnny tried not to think about that. Instead he slowly lowered himself to his knees until the inscription was at eye level. From the left-hand pocket of his parka he took out the flashlight. He examined the first *ye*, but there was nothing odd about it. The letters were no more deeply cut than the others around them. Johnny tried the other *ye*, and this time his heart jumped. Around the word was a faint ragged line—a crack in the stonework. It looked as if the crack had been smeared over with plaster at one time, but wind and weather had eaten most of the plaster away. Johnny dug his hand into the pocket on the right side of his parka and pulled out the screwdriver. Holding the flashlight steady with his left hand, he poked at the crack. Immediately more plaster flaked away. The crack got wider, the tip of the screwdriver sank in deeper, and Johnny wiggled it around to widen the crack. All around the wandering circle he went, poking and prying and loosening. Tiny gray flakes fluttered down onto the ledge. Excitedly Johnny pulled back his right hand, and he stabbed as hard as he could. The tip of the screwdriver sank in an inch or more. Johnny pried, and the slab started to move. But the work would take two hands, and so he laid down the flashlight. Now he heaved with all his strength, and the thick slab of stone fell out onto the ledge with a *chunk*. Excited, Johnny snatched up his flashlight and peered into the ragged hole. He expected to see a legal-looking bundle tied with red ribbon, or a metal strongbox with a padlock on it.

But what he saw was neither of these. It was a small square can. The label said Herb-Ox Bouillon Cubes.

Johnny could have cried. Was this it then? Was this what he had come up here for, in the snow, in the dark, in the cold? One last flickering hope remained. Maybe the can contained microfilm, and the will was printed on it. Impatiently Johnny pried the lid off. Inside were little cubes wrapped in gold-colored foil. He unwrapped the first one. And the second and the third and all the rest. Chicken bouillon cubes.

With a violent heave, Johnny hurled the can off the ledge and listened as it clattered on the pavement below. He felt like the biggest fool who ever walked on two legs. By now the professor and his grandparents would be frantic with worry. The police were probably out beating the bushes around Duston Heights. Police dogs were sniffing for him in the woods outside town. And when he came back to them, what could he bring? Bouillon cubes.

Johnny knelt there, facing the wall. He wanted to cry, but the tears would not come. His mind was racing through all the possibilities. If Mrs. Woodley really was a witch, maybe she had changed the will into a can of Herb-Ox Bouillon Cubes. It was an idiotic thought, but right now the idea seemed about as reasonable as anything else that he could come up with. He shook his head and heaved a deep, shuddering sigh. The game was over. He would just have to go home. Glumly Johnny picked up the flashlight, stuffed the screwdriver into his pocket, and carefully pulled himself to his feet. Edging to the right, he reached out in the dark and felt for handholds and footholds among the tangled vines. Now he was making his way down, and he found, strangely enough, that he was thinking of hot cereal. He wanted to be in a nice warm room, in his pajamas and bathrobe, eating a steaming bowl of Gramma's oatmeal, with maple syrup and brown sugar and cream.

But when his foot touched the ground Johnny turned around. It seemed to be snowing harder. He wanted to get away, far from this awful place as quickly as he could. With a sinking heart, he realized that he would probably have to go back down through the crypt. There was a high, spike-topped iron fence around the estate, and he didn't feel up to scaling it. But as he turned back toward the dark doorway of the chapel, he saw something. Someone was coming down the steps toward him with arms outstretched. A figure in a yellow raincoat. A figure with hollow mummy eyes and a withered mummy face and clawlike mummy hands. Moving with an awful, tottering, unsteady gait, it came toward him.

CHAPTER FIFTEEN

Johnny screamed. He dropped the flashlight and ran blindly into the night as the snow swirled around him. Now he saw the vast shadow of the old mansion looming up before him. He could make out its blank, forbidding wall of stone towering up into the night. Madly Johnny raced along the wall, looking for a door. He wished he could see where he was going! It was pitch black out, and if a pit suddenly opened up before his feet, he would fall right in. Now the wall was turning. Johnny turned too. He had seen a couple of tall windows in heavy stone frames. But no doors, none at all. . . .

Then he saw it. A low door, half-sunk in the ground. He could hide till morning, and maybe the awful thing would go away. Johnny was filled with terror. He didn't want to die. He didn't want to end up like Chad. No, not like that. . . .

He was at the door. He shook the knob, but it held tight. Johnny shut his eyes and screeched: *"Let me in!* LET ME IN!*"* He pounded on the door. Horribly he felt something clawing weakly at his back. Was Chad trying to stop him from entering the building? Was he trying to help him? The thought raced madly through Johnny's brain. *Oh, God, oh, God, please* . . . Johnny gasped, and then, incredibly, the door opened. He did not stop to wonder why but plunged in and slammed it shut behind him.

He had escaped. But what had he escaped into? There had been a little light outside, but there was none at all here. Groping like a blind man, Johnny found a stair railing. Up he went, shuffling, one step at a time. At the top he found another door and opened it. A musty, shut-up smell rushed out to meet him. While Johnny was wondering what kind of room he was in, thunder rumbled overhead, and lightning flashed. For a brief instant he saw a huge kitchen with a long counter running down the middle, and copper kettles hanging from a rack overhead. At the far end of the kitchen was another door. He felt like a rat caught in a maze, or the pinball in a pinball machine. Lightning flashed again, and this time Johnny made a dash for it.

The heavy door boomed behind him. Now he was in the dark again. But as he felt his way along, his hand rubbed the top of something smooth—a table, probably.

Again there was a sudden flash of lightning in the three tall windows, and Johnny had a brief glimpse of an enormous paneled dining room. A table as long as a bowling alley ran down the middle, and rows of high-backed chairs flanked it. He was standing by a low side table, and on the table were . . . candles! Just what he needed! Now, if only he could find some matches! Blindly he groped across the dusty surface of the table. He heard things fall, and something rolled off the table and smashed on the floor. Then his hand closed over a small box. He pushed at the end, and it slid in. A match-box! Johnny's fumbling fingers found small stick matches. He felt the side of the box and *br-rr-rip!* went the match. A pinpoint of sulfurous light flared, and with a trembling hand Johnny lit the candle. Ah, blessed light! Johnny tottered forward across the dusty floor. The candlelight glimmered in a row of tall mirrors to his right. His shadowy reflection made Johnny jump. He stumbled this way and that, holding the candle up and straining his eyes till his head ached. There had to be a way out—a main entrance, or another side entrance . . . something, anything! Johnny gritted his teeth. He would get out if it killed him. Ghosts or no ghosts, mummies or no . . .

A silvery voice began to sing, high-pitched and mock-ing:

> A tisket, a tasket,
> A will in a wicker basket!

and then:

I found it, I found it,
I green and yellow found it!

The voice died away. Then Johnny glanced at his candle. The flame was burning blue! The Guardian was here! For a second he went numb with terror, but he summoned up all his willpower and forced himself to stumble ahead across the dusty floor. He pushed open a set of tall French doors and crossed another room. He paused and looked this way and that in utter bewilderment. And then the walls of the room began to shake. A cobwebbed chandelier trembled overhead, and its thousands of glass pendants set up a loud, alarmed clattering. Panicked, Johnny rushed off to the right. He had seen another set of French doors there. The walls and the floor continued to pitch and heave, like the deck of a ship in a storm. Johnny slipped to his knees. The flame of the candle wavered but did not go out. Staggering to his feet, he made it to the doors, shoved them open, and stepped out onto a curved stone balcony. In the distance, beyond the chapel and the iron fence, he saw headlights. A car! But whose car, and what were they doing? Then he turned and looked up. A row of ornamental stone doodads ran along the top of the mansion —vases, balls, obelisks with carved swags and lions' heads on them. And they were all lit with a ghostly green fire that flickered and made haloes in the air.

A sudden gust of wind blew snow at Johnny, and his candle went out. But then lightning flashed, and Johnny

) 150 (

saw that he was standing next to something—a huge statue of a warrior in chain mail. The warrior wore over his suit of mail a surcoat with a Maltese cross on it. The warrior's face was grim, and he had a long drooping mustache. His enormous arm clutched the hilt of his sword, and he seemed to be just about to draw it from the scabbard. On the base of the statue a name was carved. Johnny had seen it only for a tenth of a second, but he had been able to make it out. It was a name he knew from history books: *Godfrey de Bouillon.*

Godfrey de Bouillon
Herb-Ox Bouillon Cubes

Johnny's brain turned somersaults. It spun like a merry-go-round gone crazy. What if? What if he had found the will? Had he thrown away the greatest clue of all? Could he still . . .

As if in answer, the building rocked. It shook as if the walls were made of cardboard, and pieces of stone, roof tiles, and bricks from the chimney stack came raining down. The room that Johnny had just left was already on fire. Huge jagged cracks had opened in the floor, and red flames were shooting up through them. Again the mansion shook. The enormous statue tottered on its base and then went crashing through the railing of the balcony. Johnny clung to a carved pilaster and prayed: *Jesus, Mary, and Joseph, hear our prayers and grant our petitions, Jesus, Mary, and—*

Something hit him in the head, and he blacked out.

CHAPTER SIXTEEN

When Johnny woke up he found that he was lying in a hospital bed. It was daytime, and cold winter light was streaming in through large windows. Next to him, sitting in an armchair by the bed, was the professor. He was wearing an egg-stained brown sweater, and he was smoking one of his eternal black-and-gold cigarettes as he grinned broadly at Johnny.

"So!" he exclaimed in a pretend-gruff voice. "You've decided to favor us with your presence at last! And about time too! How do you feel?"

Johnny was still dazed and uncertain. He didn't know quite how he felt. But now he realized that there was something on his head. He reached up and touched the stiff white cloth of a bandage. Then he remembered being out on the balcony and getting hit on the head.

"Have I been . . . ?" he began, but he found he was having trouble putting words together. He felt vaguely dizzy, and when he moved, a throbbing headache started, just above his left eye.

"Yes, you have been *indeed!*" said the professor, smiling gently. "You have been totally unconscious for about two days. It's a concussion—no, don't worry, it's not fatal. I had one myself once, when I was hit in the head with a shell casing at the Battle of the Argonne Forest. You'll be up and around in a few days. In case you're wondering, you're in a hospital in North Conway, New Hampshire. It's the nearest one we could find. North Conway is a rich little town where people come to ski and drink and sit around and be bored. You should see the overpriced dump that *I'm* staying in. It's a fake Swiss chalet, with cuckoo clocks and everything. Fortunately it isn't the skiing season yet, or the room would cost me half my year's salary at the college. And the bed is lumpy too—would you believe it?"

The professor crabbed on. Johnny grinned and listened appreciatively. He knew that this was cheerful crabbing, a sign the professor was in a good mood. And as the professor talked Johnny found that the cobwebs in his head were clearing away. He remembered why he had come up here—the will, the reward, and everything. He thought about Mrs. Woodley, and Chad, and Godfrey de Bouillon. There were a million questions that he wanted to ask.

"Is . . . is the mansion all burned down?"

The professor nodded. "It is indeed. Burned to a nice crunchy crisp. It's just a heap of rubble now. But it was still going strong when Fergie and I arrived on the scene. We—"

"*Fergie?*" exclaimed Johnny, interrupting. "What was he doing up here?"

The professor eyed Johnny sardonically. "He came up here with me to rescue you. And you will have to admit, my friend, that you needed some rescuing. You were lying in the bushes near the mansion when we found you. The mansion was going like . . . well, it was going like a house afire. Flames shooting out of all the windows, walls crashing down all over the place. Well, Fergie—or Byron, as I prefer to call him—Byron and I fought our way in, and it was hot, let me tell you. But we got to you and pulled you free just before the whole bloody wall came down—blooey, crash, bam!—right where you'd been not a moment before. How about that, eh?"

Johnny was silent. So he had missed death by just that much.

"Mrs. Woodley probably started that fire," the professor went on as he lit another cigarette. "And she started the earthquake and the lightning and all the other fireworks that helped to wreck the mansion. She did it by remote control, with the aid of a very strange witchcraftical box that she found when she was nosing around out at the estate, looking for the will. And how do I know all this? Because of a diary that was found in the bedroom of the dear sweet departed old—"

"*Departed?* You mean she's—"

The professor nodded solemnly. "Yes, I'm afraid so. Kindly old Mrs. Woodley, the proprietor of the friendly Squam House, has gone to glory . . . or she has gone to someplace, at any rate. They found her in her bedroom, slumped over that witch box I told you about. Heart attack, I'm told. If she were alive, she'd have a lot to answer for. According to her diary, she did in Chad Glomus and three other people she found poking around the estate. She was obsessed with her brother's will—terrified somebody would find it and it would turn out that she had been cut off without a nickel. Mrs. Woodley was a clever old bat, I'll give her that. Like you, she figured out the "Staunton Harold" part of the puzzle. But she couldn't get any further. Did you manage to figure it all out? The tea shop sign and everything?"

Johnny frowned. "Sort of. Only I didn't know it. When I got to the last clue, I didn't realize what it was. I thought I'd got rooked. Do you wanta hear about it?"

The professor nodded. And as he smoked, Johnny told him about the inscription over the chapel door. He explained about the two *ye*'s and the can of bouillon cubes and the statue of Godfrey de Bouillon. ". . . and so I think the will has got to be inside of the statue," Johnny concluded. "I mean, it stands to reason that that's where it'd be. Do . . . do you think you could have the police go and find out if it really is there?"

The professor considered this. "Hmm. Well, I guess we'd better have them investigate the matter. The mansion is just a ruin now, as I said before. But the statue is probably there somewhere in the rubble. Godfrey de Bouillon. Huh! Well, you know, while I was waiting for you to recover, I read the little guidebook that you had in your coat pocket. And I did notice the part about the Nine Worthies."

"Yeah," said Johnny. "Who were they, anyway?"

The professor smiled smugly, as he always did when he knew something that somebody else didn't know. "They were sort of a Hit Parade of warriors and heroes of the ancient world," he said. "Let's see, there's Joshua, David, Judas Maccabeus, Hector, Alexander . . . um, don't rush me. . . . Ah, yes! And there's Julius Caesar, and King Arthur, good old Charlemagne, and of course our soupy old friend, Godfrey de Bouillon, the noted knight and leader of the Crusaders. That's nine, isn't it? And in case you're interested, I also know all about the inscription over the chapel door and what it means. But I'll bore you with that some other time. We have more important things to discuss now."

The professor's jaunty, kidding manner disappeared. He grew serious and solemn. "Did you know that Fergie and I were arrested?" he asked.

Johnny was stunned. "You *were*? What for?"

"For arson, trespassing, and attempted burglary . . . those are all the charges, I think, though there may be more. You see, as soon as we had dragged you away from the burning building, we heard this incredible racket. It was the firemen and policemen bashing open the gate in the fence to get in! Yes, indeedy! There must've been about eight fire trucks and I don't know how many police cars, and, luckily, there was also an ambulance. But when the cops found us, they figured we had set the fire. Can you imagine! I mean, what a bunch of ninnies!"

Johnny was worried. "Are . . . are you gonna hafta go to jail?"

The professor chuckled and shook his head. "No, we aren't going to jail. You see, in a case of this sort the owners of the property would have to prefer charges. As you know, the owners are the surviving members of the Glomus family. And when they found out about Mrs. Woodley—Mr. Glomus's sister that was—and the *thing* that was discovered in the ruins of the mansion, and all the other *things* that were scattered all over the grounds of the estate . . . well, they were in no mood to prefer charges against *anybody*!"

Johnny's mouth dropped open. "Things? What things?"

The professor smiled wryly and flicked the ash off the end of his cigarette. "Oh, not much. Just a few hard-to-explain items. First, the police found a mummified body in the ruins of the house. From the clothes, and from the ring and the wallet and the other personal belongings, they have concluded, reluctantly, that it is the body of Chad Glomus. They're going to have to consult dental records to be sure, but for myself I have no doubt that it's the young man who disappeared early in October. Nobody can figure out how the body came to be—"

"I didn't tell you everything," said Johnny, interrupting. "I mean, Fergie and me, we were with Chad just before he died. We . . . we kind of wanted to keep it a secret."

"Yes," said the professor quietly. "I know. Fergie has already spilled the beans. And I must say, it is quite an amazing tale. There's more too. The police decided to do a thorough search of all the buildings on the estate. And what do you suppose they found in Mr. Glomus's mausoleum? The bodies of three other people who disappeared up here during the last few years. They were mummies too, and they were standing up, stiff as boards, against a wall. They were all local characters— two old derelicts and a woman who lived in a tar-paper shack near Mount Chocorua. And they all must've made the mistake of breaking into the estate and nosing around. Mrs. Woodley found out, and that was the end of *them*!"

The professor paused for breath. He heaved a deep sigh and folded his arms. "Well, now, would you like to see what the newspapers have been making of all this?"

Without waiting for an answer, the professor reached

down beside his armchair, picked up a thick sheaf of newspapers, and threw them onto Johnny's bed. They were all copies of the Manchester *Union-Leader*, the most popular paper in New Hampshire. Johnny looked at the headline that was lying on top. HORROR MUMMIES IN CEREAL MAGNATE'S TOMB. He flipped to the next one and read THE WITCH OF KANCAMAGUS CENTER? Another said WAS CHAD MURDERED? MYSTERY DEEPENS.

Johnny flipped quickly through the stack. "Oh, my gosh," he said. It was not much of a comment, but it was the only one he could come up with.

"You see?" said the professor, cocking his head to one side and grinning in that know-it-all way that he had. "This whole shindig has given the Glomus family some very undesirable publicity. And as far as I can tell, they would like to have it all hushed up as quickly as possible. So unless I miss my guess, they're not going to charge the three of us with anything. There will, however, be an inquest. There *has* to be when four bodies are discovered. And you know something? I would *love* to know what those crime-lab clowns are going to say about those mummies! I wonder what sort of silly, trashy, pseudoscientific flummery they will—"

"Hey!" said Johnny, interrupting again. He sat up suddenly, and then, as a sharp searing pain slashed through his head, he sank back onto the pillow. "I . . . we . . . we have to do something! Right now! We have to get the cops to go out to the mansion an' look inside of that statue to see if the will's there! I mean . . . I mean,

Gramma's sick, an' if I don't get the reward money right away, she might *die*! Please, professor! Can you get 'em to do something, right now? Can you?"

The professor put his hand over his face. "For Pete's sake!" he said through his fingers. "Is *that* why you went after the will? John, as Jimmy Durante would say, you been laborin' under a misprehamprehension! Your grandmother isn't dying! The operation was a success, a complete and unqualified success! Of course, she's no spring chicken, but still . . . good grief, why didn't you *ask* somebody?"

A tear trickled down Johnny's cheek. "I was scared. I mean . . . I mean, I got all this bad news, about Dad and all, and I thought the world was comin' to an end! And then I found that letter from the undertakers, so I thought . . ."

The professor nodded somberly. "I see it all now. What a comedy of errors! John, my lad, do you know what that letter was probably about?"

Johnny sniffled. He took a tissue from a box on the table and blew his nose. "Nope. What was it about?"

The professor grinned. "A few years ago your grandfather's brother Willie died. He was next door to being a bum, and after the funeral Willie's wife wrote a check to the funeral parlor, and the check bounced. Well, the undertakers had a fit, and they got after Willie's widow, and she went to your grampa for help. There was a big fight in your grampa's family about who would foot the bill, and, well, your grampa finally persuaded his other brother, Vic, to pay it. Vic is a filthy rich farmer up in Menominee, Wisconsin, and he could afford it. So I suspect—though I'm not absolutely sure—that the letter you saw was just a note from somebody at the funeral parlor thanking your grampa because he had managed to pry the money out of his tight-fisted brother. I'd be willing to bet that that's all there was to that ridiculous letter. And next time if you have any doubts about a letter's contents, steam the bloody thing open and peek inside, for heaven's sake!" With an exasperated "Hmph!" the professor ground out his cigarette in the ashtray. He dug another one out of his pocket and lit it.

Johnny's lower lip began to tremble. Tears were rolling down his cheeks. "I . . . I'm sorry," he stammered. "I didn't know, I . . ."

The professor was shocked—he hadn't meant to make Johnny cry. With an agonized look on his face he jumped out of his chair and rushed over to Johnny's bed. He took the cigarette from his mouth and, after looking about distractedly, he dunked it in a glass of water that stood on the bedside table. When he turned back to Johnny, the professor's eyes were filled with tears.

"Oh, John!" he cried as he seized the bedsheet in his hands and began to twist it. "*Please* don't cry! I'm just a cranky old man, and I can't help sounding grumpy sometimes! It's one of my many faults."

Johnny smiled and dried his eyes with a tissue. "It's okay, Professor," he said, sniffling. "I just feel . . . kinda weird right now, and it's easy to cry. And I'm happy I'm not gonna be alone in the world. That makes me wanta cry too."

"Well, you mustn't!" said the professor, and he smiled a weak, wan, half-joking smile. Still twisting the bed-sheet, he stared hard at Johnny. "Look," he said in a grave but gentle voice. "I . . . I think I understand why you did what you did. And in connection with that I have something to tell you. I was going to save this for later, but . . . your dad has been found." Johnny's eyes opened wide and he exclaimed, "When—" But the professor replied quickly, "I'll give you the details later; I just wanted you to know he's all right. But even if he hadn't been found, and even if both your grandfather and your grandmother were to die, I'd still be there to take care of you. I've never had any children of my own, but if they'd let me, I'd adopt you. I'm only seventy, you know. My father made it to a hundred and three, and his father was ninety-eight when the horse he was riding threw him. You don't need to worry about ever being an orphan."

Johnny was going to say something in answer to the professor, but the old man turned away quickly and walked to the window. As he stood glaring out at the snow-covered hillside he harrumphed loudly several times and clicked his false teeth in and out. The professor hated it when he got emotional in front of other people. Then he sat down and talked with Johnny about his father.

Johnny stayed at the hospital in North Conway for a week. During that time the professor went on living at the expensive hotel, and Fergie stayed with him for a day or two. Together they visited Johnny at the hospital every day. Finally Fergie gave a statement to the local police, and then he went home on the train to Duston Heights. After the police got statements from Johnny and the professor, an inquest was held. The coroner's jury decided that Chad and the other three had died "of unexplained causes."

Acting on information from Johnny, the police went out to the Glomus estate, poked around in the ruins, and found the broken, charred statue of Godfrey de Bouillon. By tapping with hammers they discovered that the base of the statue was hollow. A sliding panel of stone could be pulled back, and inside the base of the statue they found . . . a small heap of ashes. The statue had fallen into the basement of the burning building, and the heat there had been so intense that it had been like a brick oven. The will of Mr. H. Bagwell Glomus was gone forever.

Johnny was unhappy when he heard this, but now that he knew his grandmother wasn't dying, the will had become far less important to him. The professor merely repeated what he had said when he heard that Mrs. Woodley had died—*Good riddance to bad rubbish!*

After a week the professor drove Johnny home to Duston Heights. When he arrived, he got lots of hugs and kisses from his grandmother, who was bustling around like her old self now. And Grampa shook the professor's hand so many times that the professor finally had to tell him to stop.

That evening Fergie came to visit Johnny. Despite their chats at the hospital, they had not had a chance to have a really private conversation. So, the first chance Johnny got, he took Fergie up to his room, and they had a long and excited gabfest. Later, while they played chess, it occurred to Johnny that he had at least gotten one good thing out of this whole mess: He had found a new friend.

The next day Johnny went back to school. He tried to pretend that nothing had happened, but everyone had read about Johnny's adventure in the newspapers. They all wanted to ask him questions, and some kids even wanted his autograph. So, by the time he left school at three fifteen, his nerves were thoroughly frazzled. As he turned onto Fillmore Street and started walking toward his house, he found that he had yet another jolt in store for him on this busy, trying day. There was a car parked in front of his house, a sleek black limousine with a chauffeur at the wheel. A wild thought leaped into Johnny's mind: Could it be his dad?

But it wasn't his dad. Johnny's grandmother met him at the door. She was clearly quite upset and nervous as she explained that there was a lady waiting for him in the parlor. Johnny felt let down, but he was still curious. Who could it be? When he walked in, he saw, seated on the couch, a tall, haughty-looking old woman. She wore an expensive flowered silk dress and a pearl necklace. Rings glittered on her fingers, and her iron-gray hair was arranged in a ripply permanent wave. When she saw Johnny, the woman smiled. Surprisingly it was not merely a polite smile but one of genuine warmth and friendliness.

"How are you!" she said, rising and holding out her hand. "My name is Annabelle Glomus. My husband was H. Bagwell Glomus. You've heard of him, I believe?" Mrs. Glomus's eyes gleamed with amusement. And to Johnny's amazement she winked at him!

"I, uh . . . I, uh . . ." Johnny began, but he couldn't get any further than that. He was really tongue-tied.

Still smiling, Mrs. Glomus sat down again. Johnny sank into a seat next to her. What on earth did she want?

Then Mrs. Glomus picked up her large patent-leather purse. She opened it up and took out a checkbook and a gold-plated fountain pen. As Johnny watched she began to write out a check.

"I have heard about your exploits up in New Hampshire," she said with a faint ringe of amusement in her voice. "And I must say that I'm sorry, profoundly sorry, that the famous Glomus puzzle led you on a wild-goose chase and almost turned out very badly indeed. For myself I never thought there was a will at all. I believed the puzzle was merely something dreamed up by my late husband to drive us all mad. But now that it seems there was a will, I must say that I am *extremely* glad it was destroyed. At my age I have no stomach for bickering. It was those greedy sons of mine who advertised in the paper and hounded me into putting up the reward money. They both thought that the will would make them richer—though I could never figure out why. I mean, my dear sweet late husband was capable of doing a lot of strange things. He *might* have left my sons a bundle. On the other hand, he might have left his money to the Ku Klux Klan or to a cat hospital in New South Wales. So, on the whole, I think we're much better off with no will at all. But since you did find the will—that is, you found out where it was hidden—and fair is fair, I want you to have this."

When she had gotten out this last sentence, Mrs. Glomus tore the check out of her checkbook and handed it to Johnny. It was made out to him, for ten thousand dollars.

Johnny was stunned. He tried to say something, but once again words failed him. While he was stammering, Mrs. Glomus stood up and started to leave. At the door she paused and turned back to him once more.

"Good day to you, young man. I hope you do something enjoyable with the money. And I hope you will realize that not all of the members of the Glomus family are like my late husband's sister. Some of us are quite sane and reasonable . . . and nice people too." And with that, Mrs. Glomus turned and swept grandly out of the room, leaving Johnny alone with the check in his hands.

As soon as Johnny had recovered from the shock he ran out into the kitchen to tell his grandmother and grandfather.

"Well, my Lord!" exclaimed Gramma, holding the check up and peering at it in astonishment. "Who woulda thought it? I mean, heavens to Betsy, *who?*" She handed it back to Johnny and shook her head solemnly. "Well, my boy," she said, putting her hand on Johnny's arm, "this has really been a time for s'prises for us all lately! Do you think the s'prises are all over with? For now, I mean?"

Johnny said that he figured they were. But he was wrong. In fact, he had just barely finished speaking when there was a loud squeal of brakes outside. His first thought was that it was Mrs. Glomus coming to take the check back. But when he rushed out to the bay window in the parlor, he saw that the car that had just pulled up was khaki-colored. On its door words were stenciled in white paint: U.S. ARMY. Then Johnny saw the door on the passenger side open. Somebody got out. With a joyful whoop Johnny rushed to the front door and tore it open. He galloped across the porch and down the front steps. Standing next to the car was a man in a gray U.S. Air Force uniform. Battle ribbons and medals covered the left side of the man's uniform jacket, and on his cap and shoulders were the insignia of a captain. His face was craggy, seamed with wrinkles, and deeply tanned. But in spite of the tan, the man's face looked pinched and worn, as if he had just been through a bad time. Nonetheless he was smiling broadly and holding out his arms to Johnny. Rushing forward with happy yells and yips and whoops, Johnny threw himself against the man and hugged him tight. The man hugged him back, and now he was crying. The two of them just stood there, holding each other for a long time.

ABOUT THE AUTHOR

JOHN BELLAIRS is the critically acclaimed and bestselling author of many gothic novels for young readers, including THE CURSE OF THE BLUE FIGURINE; THE SPELL OF THE SORCERER'S SKULL; THE TREASURE OF ALPHEUS WINTERBORN; THE DARK SECRET OF WEATHEREND; THE EYES OF THE KILLER ROBOT; THE MUMMY, THE WILL, AND THE CRYPT; THE REVENGE OF THE WIZARD'S GHOST, all published in the Bantam Skylark line. A resident of Haverhill, Massachusetts, Mr. Bellairs has also written another suspense thriller for children, THE LAMP FROM THE WARLOCK'S TOMB, which will be available in a Bantam Skylark edition in the spring of 1989.